LEAH SWANN lives in Melbourne with her husband and two children. She has worked as a public relations manager, journalist and speech writer.

Bearings is her first book.

LEAH SWANN

BEARINGS

Published by Affirm Press in 2011
1 Jacksons Road, Mulgrave VIC 3170
www.affirmpress.com.au

Text copyright © Leah Swann
All rights reserved. No part of this publication may be reproduced without prior permission of the publisher.

National Library of Australia Cataloguing-in-Publication entry
Swann, Leah
Bearings / Leah Swann
978-0-9807904-2-9 (pbk)
Series: Long Story Shorts; 5
Fiction – Short Stories
A823.4

Designed and illustrated by Dean Gorissen/Room44
Printed in Australia by Griffin Press

Bearings is part of the Long Story Shorts initiative, a commitment by Affirm Press to publish a series of six individual collections of stories.

To the memory of my grandparents, Fred and Gladys Swann, who did so much for all of us.

CONTENTS

Street Sweeper 9
The Singles Club 22
All Your Mothers 40
Lovest Thou Me 53
Silver Hands: A Novella 71
Slow to Learn 145
The Easter Hare 164
The Ringwood Madonna 177

STREET SWEEPER

YOU'LL REMEMBER THIS DAY your dog Winston dies, this day and this night, but right now the afternoon is fresh and untouched by future events. Here you are on the concrete steps, in front of a shabby weatherboard: Mathew Greene at fourteen, with a skateboard under one arm, the other filled with the shaggy warmth of Winston.

Listless, you feel in need of something. But it won't be found in the kitchen – where your mother, Molly, makes jam with Bridget like it's an hilarious science experiment – nor downstairs in the mad slurry of Monopoly money and scone crumbs left by the children. You're too old to play.

Greene senior, the father who gave you Winston on your third birthday, is not here. He married someone else and lives in America with new children. It's no one's fault; it's just the way things are. Last time he visited, you played footy on the street. You told me it was the best hour of your life.

You hear the women's conversation through the open front door. You're dimly aware that this jam-making business is somehow attached to your mother's need to be accepted by the brigade of Other Mothers. You can't stand her ostentatious efforts. If she cut off her dreadlocks and removed a few earrings, she might get further. But you can't say such things. You don't want to.

'My goodness, if my mother could see me now,' Molly says. Knives slash and chop on the cutting boards.

'My mother didn't make jam either,' says Bridget. 'But it's a good antidote to the madness of modern life.'

'These mandarins are appalling.'

'Not enough rain.'

'Satisfying to make them into jam, though,' says Molly.

There are cigarette butts in the geranium pot by the steps, Marlboro Lights, Molly's brand. Citrus infuses the air like a pungent teabag. Hearing a cork pop, you know Molly's opened a bottle of wine and your chest kinks with anger. The one bright spot of your day is the evening walk, when you and Molly and your little brother and sister walk the dog. It will be awful if she's drunk — and she could well be drunk by then.

You're hungry but you can't bear to return to the kitchen. You don't want to enter that warm, womanly fug of jam and alcohol and Bridget's cleavage. Now they're testing the jam on a cold saucer; you can hear your mother worrying that it's too runny.

You're itching for something. You don't know what, though later you wonder if you were waiting for the car that screamed around the corner, the car that killed Winston, and the girl in velvet hipsters who tumbled out of the driver's seat, weeping.

You set out to skate from the letterbox to the fire hydrant and back. Winston follows, arthritic and shambling. You've already skated two lengths before the dog's made it to the nature strip to relieve himself. He's wandered out on the road when you hear the car's engine too close and too fast.

'Winston!'

The great bushy head lifts to attention, his eyes obscured by a long fringe of grey and white hair. He doesn't move.

'Winston, come here!'

Ponderous, as if moving through water, the dog raises a paw like a Clydesdale hoof and puts it down again. The red Astra hurtles around the bend. Brakes squealing, the car smashes into Winston and sends him soaring along the road. The Astra screeches to a stop, and the driver climbs out. She's already crying.

Winston must be dead. You run to him and pick up his front and back paws. You're dragging him to the kerb when you see that he's split open – his guts are rolling out. Behind you, the girl gives a short scream.

'Don't worry,' you hear yourself say. 'Don't worry about it. I'll get a spade. I'll clean it up.'

The girl's shoulders are shaking. 'Oh my God, oh my God! I'm so sorry.'

'You can go home, if you want,' you say. *Please go home. Please go. I can't stand it.*

The girl's eyes are dripping black over her lovely face: she's the kind of girl you'd be in awe of in other circumstances. A navel-diamanté winks up at you from her flat belly, making you hot and uncomfortable.

'No, let me help,' she pleads.

'*I* want to do it,' you say. 'Please.'

'Do you want me to go?'

'Yes.'

Running down the driveway, through the noisy kitchen to the back door, you find the spade and walk back through the kitchen. The wine bottle is almost empty. A foaming pot of gold on the stove threatens to boil over, guarded by a giggling Molly with her wine glass and wooden spoon; Bridget's ladling the first batch into washed jars. A row of finished jars sits on the windowsill, back-lit by sunshine, each one full of a dense and radiant orange.

'What the hell's Matt doing with a spade?' you hear Bridget say.

'God knows. Spot of gardening, perhaps?' says Molly. A gale of laughter follows you up the driveway and you think to yourself, *bitch*; but only minutes later she's out there beside you, helping you, proving you wrong.

When you tell me of the evening walks your voice is tender. How the littlies hold hands and walk in front, hauling Winston on the leash, while your mother's beside you, deftly winding the conversation this way and that way, and listening intently to whatever you say about school, dreams, football, skateboards – even girls. You only notice this skilfulness in retrospect. But you bask in her attention; these walks are when you love her best.

She knows how to handle you. When she arrives on the street that unforgettable spring day, Winston spread over the bitumen like the Pro Hart carpet advertisement, she says in a low voice: 'What we need here, Mathew, is a box. Run across to the Stuarts' and see if they have one, as big as you can find.'

Bridget is standing nearby. Molly leans over and says something to her you can't hear. Glad to leave the scene for a moment, you hand Molly the spade and dash over to the neighbours' house.

Molly must have worked like lightning, because by the time you get back most of the dog is in an oversized pillow-slip and another, smaller slip. The small one has a faded Thomas the Tank Engine print on it, the one you insisted on having on until you were ten. You set the box onto the nature strip and lift the sacks into the box. Each is knotted, so no furry vestiges of poor Winston protrude. Blood's staining the cotton, fast.

'I think it's best if Georgia and Stefan don't see this,' says Molly, wiping sweat from her forehead.

'I'll take them for tea at my house,' says Bridget.

Once you've carried the box to the backyard, you go inside to clean up. In the bathroom, you wash your hands and face. There are voices outside, followed by Bridget's car driving away. In the mirror you see a whisker poking out of your chin and yank it out with your thumb and forefinger. You walk into the bedroom. Sinking into the bed, your hand stretches by habit to feel Winston's head and swishes through empty air. You lean forward all the way and press your eye sockets into your kneecaps and cry. Tears soak your jeans.

Eventually you go back to the garden where Molly is busily digging under the old mandarin tree. She looks small and skinny with the apron – donned for jam-making – still hanging off her unmotherly form, dust-blonde dreadlocks tucked behind earlobes bristling with silver. There's a tattoo of a sun on her right bicep. The arm that stirred the pot. The arm that dug the grave. It's shaking with effort.

'Let me do that, Mum,' you say.

She hands you the spade gratefully, and wipes at the muck and tears smearing her face.

Later, there will be a memorial service. Georgia and Stefan will toss flowers onto the grave and say poems in Winston's memory. Right now, their absence lets the two of you cry freely. All is quiet, save for the sound of tears and dirt falling over blood-stained pillowslips.

'He was a good dog,' chokes Molly, when it's almost done.

'The best,' you say, and put your arm around her and again you notice the slightness of her, this woman so big in your life.

During the night you can't stop thinking about Winston's body coming apart. You want to stop but your mind keeps going back to it, probing it like a finger on a scab.

You try to think of the mandarins and the hands of the women, their chopping blades, sectioning, stripping, peeling. Dozens of mandarins slashed in half, their dry gold bellies face-up. Pips and pith and shells of orange skin sitting in heaps between the blue packets of sugar. The driver's face comes to mind, and you wonder if she's awake too, disturbed by killing a dog. Despite your efforts, you keep seeing red guts and other stuff, brown and shiny and sausage-like, on the hard road.

Finally you fall into a hot, fitful sleep, only to be woken by the harsh noise of a street sweeper. The vast mechanical brooms whirr through the quiet, breaking it up into so many shards.

When you put on your runners, you slip through the bedroom window and out onto the street. It's late. You pad along, jogging lightly. Cold moonlight spilling over a blossom tree makes it so sharply beautiful, so unearthly – it takes you by surprise. You will always remember its fragrance, its stillness, its lambent white blossoms.

Up the road comes the street sweeper. You avert your eyes from the glaring gold lights, sitting on the truck like upturned jam jars, but nothing can block the noise. It passes you slowly, a moving edifice of brutal efficiency, its raucous vacuum strong enough to suck up a house brick or a dead possum. Even bits of Winston. But Molly did such a good job, there's barely a trace of Winston left; every piece has been wrapped and buried. At least he was saved from that.

As you hurry back along the street to your house, you see a light on in Molly's room. Leaping through your window and sliding into bed, your heart thumps. She's talking to someone on the phone. At this time of night it could only be America. Molly's voice is too muffled to hear what she's saying. Maybe the bad school report. Maybe Winston.

When the conversation ends, you creep into your mother's bedroom. She's in her singlet top and pyjama pants. Her eyes are pink.

'Was that Dad?' you ask, clambering onto the bed next to her.

'Why are you still awake? Were you listening?'

'Couldn't sleep. Winston, I guess. Did you ring him?'

'No – he rang me.'

She looks through the open curtains to the night sky. Her room seems dingy with its peeling paint and op-shop dressing table. Georgia's scrappy bouquet of lavender and jasmine is wilting in the vase.

'You might as well know,' she says. 'He asked if you'd like to go and live with him. And Cady and the little ones. Become part of their family.'

You're surprised at the excitement, even joy, rising inside you. Joy with a seam of dread. It's like someone's opened a door to let in a fresh breeze. To live with him! You take a deep breath.

'It makes sense, really,' Molly says, rubbing the skin of her forehead with her thumbs. 'You're becoming a man and I don't know how to help you with that. Your father could.'

Years later, you reflect that Molly sent you away at the very moment your body grew stronger than hers; strong enough to crack open drought-dried earth with a spade. Now a grown man, you can see how such strength could have genuinely helped her maintain the house and guard the children. Had you stayed, she might have come to depend on you. Did she know she was protecting you from her own neediness, when she encouraged you – against her own feelings – to say yes to your father's offer?

Several weeks later, you say your goodbyes to Stefan and Georgia at the house. Molly's arranged for Bridget to mind them rather than go to the airport: they've been crying a lot about you going. Closing the front door, you catch sight of Stefan's little sheepskin Ugg boots left where he stepped out of them in the hallway. The toes point outwards, the way he habitually stands.

The two of you drive to the airport. After you've checked in your luggage, she waits with you. In her usual way, she keeps the conversation light and funny, teasing you about the American accent you'll inevitably acquire, and the pretty teenager she's spotted that you could 'chat up' on the plane. When the boarding call comes, she gives you a jar of mandarin marmalade.

'Give it to your Dad,' she says, and grins. 'Be sure to tell him I've been *making jam*. I'd love to see his face.'

There's a long, awkward hug, and then she holds your shoulders and looks into your eyes, and out of love for her you strive not to squirm.

'You're the best thing that ever happened to me, Mathew.'

Her eyes are bright with unshed tears and she swallows. 'Good courage, son,' she says, and laughs. 'I'm telling you what *I* need! Now remember, if you feel down just go and chat with that girl.'

Courage *is* what you need hours later, when the first real wave of homesickness hits you. Through the window lies a vast mass of sky and ocean. Your tray is flipped open in front of you with a packet of sweet biscuits, tea, and the empty dish that held the lasagne now lodged like cardboard in your stomach. The stricken face of the girl who killed Winston floats towards you, as it does sometimes; it would have been nice to talk to her about it once the shock had passed.

You stack the mess into a pile and fossick in your bag for the marmalade. Your hand closes around the cool glass jar, still sticky from where the old label has been soaked away. Drawing it out, you place it in front of you.

The jar beams on the tray, an orange beacon. Twisting the lid till it pops, you take a spoon and dip it into the marmalade, and listen to Molly and Bridget, their voices coming as though from long ago, a piece of history running through your head:

'Put the jam on this frozen saucer and we'll see if it gels.'

That's Bridget, followed by Molly: 'Oh my God, it's too runny – what will we do?'

'Keep boiling it. Just keep boiling it.'

Holding the spoon, you check the texture of the jam and find it quivers and drips in gelatinous globules onto the empty packets. She did it! A thin twist of peel dangles and glistens.

Taking another spoonful, you taste mandarins transformed by sugar and heat. Marmalade coats your tongue, thickly golden. How sweet it is, and how bitter.

THE SINGLES CLUB

That sky is cooking, thought Hiram MacLeish, glancing up from the *Dubbo Mail* as he ate his eggs. It was February and dry as a bone. Last night, Hiram had slept under a water-soaked beach towel in his studio with two fans whirring – but now, how to spend the day? The public pool offered no relief: the water was warm and slimy, and swarming with bodies. You couldn't swim, you could barely move. He preferred the river – a haunt of old times – where gum trees cast sparse shade. He liked to dive deep into the water, opening his eyes to brown flecked with sun-lit yellow: fools' gold.

Hiram checked the paper for his advertisement. There it was: *Professional artist can teach skills and appreciation to children.*

The editor had looked after him with a bold border – free of charge. Names from his school days leapt out from the classifieds: Reg Snowdon offering washing machine repairs; Melvin Bracky, who once took a stupendous mark on the footy field, running a 'third pizza free' campaign; Lily Watkins selling home-made potpourri. Mindy De Cruze. How would these people look now, these acquaintances from his youth? Who were they? Hiram clipped Mindy's ad neatly and laid it beside a scattering of paint-smeared nail parings.

The Singles Club

Tired of spending Saturday nights alone? If you are over forty and would enjoy some pleasant adult company, join us at the White Elephant this Saturday. Meals $4. Everyone Welcome.
Further details, Mindy De Cruze, Mindy's Flowers.

Lucky, thought Mindy De Cruze, that the White Elephant had a new air conditioner. Her arms were prickling into gooseflesh, and sweaty strands of hair had dried like twigs in the cold blast.

The White Elephant's main function room was nothing fancy – industrial green carpet (smelling something like petrol, wiry underfoot) and shiny 'oak' wallpaper. Mindy had hidden the Laminex tables with table cloths, and on each she placed a small glass with a pink carnation. A Chris Isaacs CD, *It's a Wicked Game*, was playing for atmosphere. She'd considered softening the neon lights with red cellophane but decided against it. When it only costs four bucks for a steaming plate of beef, gravy and potatoes, you made compromises. She knew the meal price had contributed to the success of their first meeting – over a hundred lonely hearts, from Dubbo, Gilgandra, Narromine and Dunnedoo, all from one little advertisement.

Mindy and her partner in the Singles venture, Maureen, were astonished. For the first twenty minutes it seemed disastrous – people gathered in awkward clusters, embarrassed to find they knew each other from other situations and caught in the public admission of seeking company, romance, sex. Then the brass band (hired specially) started to play, providing a talking point, and people took their places around the tables. The noise in the room grew louder, and they smiled and joked and laughed and danced. It could have been a birthday, an anniversary, a wedding. What Mindy enjoyed most was seeing her idea — so often discussed over coffee with Maureen — become reality.

Tonight, old Daphne arrived first, faintly ludicrous in vampish heels and clutching an antique cigarette holder. After her, Reg Snowdon with a mate he'd brought for moral support: a plump mechanic named Jake. There was Maureen's sister Bella, and the local clairvoyant who called herself Violet Flower. No sign of Jeffrey Winterson, the handsome headmaster of her sons' high school, who was — if Mindy would admit it — at least one reason she'd established the Singles Club. The throng thickened through the glass doors where she waited. She had reluctantly promised Hiram MacLeish that she would meet him there. She narrowed her eyes, scanning the crowd.

While Mindy looked like she was in her late thirties, with prematurely grey hair, she was closer to fifty. Her modest bust and thin hips she'd once rejected as too boyish now seemed youthful. Her olive skin was unwrinkled. She liked this emerging handsomeness, this combination of smooth skin and cropped silver hair, and felt strangely sexually confident in her ivory trouser suit.

She was revelling in this feeling, acknowledging friendly and even admiring glances, when she caught sight of someone who made her flesh crawl. Was that–? Yes, it was! Nadia Larsen. Mindy drew a startled breath. Nadia, the sleek, pearly-haired Norwegian beauty from high school could still, *after all these years*, make her twitch with jealousy. What was *she* doing here? Hadn't Nadia disappeared to Sydney decades ago, with a promising banker? That was the problem with proclaiming 'everyone welcome', thought Mindy.

Earlier in the week, Hiram had telephoned Mindy. He had seen the advertisement, and wondered if anyone could go.

'Of course,' Mindy said. 'You sound like you're over forty.' This was met with a snort of nervous laughter. 'We'd love to see you,' she added.

'Perhaps…'

'Feeling shy?' asked Mindy, encouragingly. 'Why don't you meet me at the door? Then you won't have to go in alone. What's your name?'

'Hiram. We've met before, actually. Hiram MacLeish. You know me, don't you?'

A cold bolt of dismay lodged in Mindy's gut. Of course she knew Hiram. That is, she knew Hiram's story, like everyone did; it was a public story belonging to Dubbo. Fifty years ago, Hiram had been born out of wedlock to the mayor's daughter and his illegitimacy was further complicated by his father being Aboriginal. Hiram was raised in one of Dubbo's most prominent families – his grandmother, Evelyn MacLeish, refused to send her daughter to a Sydney home for unwed mothers.

While Evelyn MacLeish may have thrown her prestigious wing over the boy, she couldn't make people forget that Hiram's green eyes gleamed from an essentially Aboriginal face. His unwitting presence magnified the town's difficult race relations: he was abused by white kids (or uncomfortably ignored, by children like Mindy) and taunted by black kids, who accused him of being a coconut. People seemed relieved when he was sent away to Yanco, an agricultural boarding school, and went on to spend his adult life as a rouseabout in the Northern Territory.

When he returned to Dubbo he rented a little studio, calling himself an artist. No one saw much of him. Mindy, like most people, didn't know he had attended a Melbourne art school and won prizes – he was just Hiram, neither whitefella nor blackfella, amiable and causing discomfort all at once.

Hiram had never married. And now here he was, opening the glass door at the White Elephant, immaculate in a chambray shirt and moleskins, eyes downcast under his Akubra hat. Mindy reached forward and grasped his hand.

She felt herself being watched by Nadia, by Maureen, by everyone in the room. She led Hiram to her table, sensing the uneasy heat around his body. *Like a force field pushing me away*, she thought, vaguely irritated, and then reminded herself that it was her job to ease him into this social occasion.

'So Hiram, what are you working on at the moment?' she asked.

'Oh, you know... The sky,' Hiram said, helplessly. He tried again: 'The way it looks in this weather.'

Hiram's newly ironed shirt reminded Mindy unexpectedly of her ex-husband. Hiram exuded that same clean scent of fabric conditioner blended with freshly washed skin: a distinct man-smell. Despite his efforts, he'd missed a triangle of azure paint on his earlobe. She struggled against an impulse to grasp the lobe and wipe it with a firm thrust of her thumb.

Towards the end of these Singles evenings, the conversation scrolled its way inevitably to failed relationships, to divorce and the death of spouses, to children no longer seen, lost money, lost homes and heartache.

Mindy told herself that this was expected, but she didn't like it. She watched Jeffrey Winterson (who had turned up after all, wearing Kouros aftershave and gold cufflinks) with the Larsen woman. Mindy had been too busy looking after Hiram to engage Jeffrey in conversation herself, so Nadia had snared him.

Hiram and Daphne were talking and smoking: Daphne from her cigarette holder and Hiram making his own (perfect cylinders emerging from rapid fingers rolling white paper, a quick flick of tongue). Mindy had a sudden flash of how Daphne must have looked in her youth, long and thin with legs crossed, dark bobbed hair cutting sharply into cheek. She was surprised that Daphne and Hiram could chat so comfortably.

For a room full of singles everyone was looking remarkably cosy. Maureen was chatting with that cuddly mechanic, Jake (who must be at least ten years her junior), and even Violet Flower was draped over a couch discussing auras with an earnest, pink-faced chap from Dunnedoo, whose corduroyed legs were tightly crossed over his crotch. Suddenly Mindy couldn't bear the whole scene. She sidled up to Maureen, gesturing.

'What is it?' said Maureen.

'I'm – so tired. Would you mind if I made a quiet exit?'

Maureen didn't look pleased. 'Okay,' she sighed. 'I'll call you in the morning.'

Stepping through the doors of the White Elephant was like stepping from one world to another: the night air was hot and real. Darkness lapped over her skin like warmed milk.

Once home, she lay on the hammock her husband had strung between two trees. How often she lay here at dusk, escaping the house full of Jason and Tony, Soundgarden and Metallica, furtive bong-smoking, beer bottles, the television full of rugby and cricket. She'd watch birds flit between branches and listen to their dwindling melodies. She had heard that in England the cellist Beatrice Harrison could start nightingales singing by playing her cello to them, and once the BBC broadcast their beautiful voices live from the meadows at midnight. When Mindy lay very still it seemed the birds enclosed her in their quiet world of wing-beats and dying song as they made their sleeping places in the branches. One time, an unwary bird had nestled right next to her face; the dull, smoky gleam of its breast-feathers close enough to touch.

As she lay gazing through a trellis of twigs she reflected that the hammock was the best present Francis ever gave her. It seemed silly now – why they had divorced. It was the oldest of plots: another woman. He'd pleaded with her, knelt at the hem of her skirt. But she had been ruthless. Embarrassed, remorseful, he gave her everything they owned, and then was too ashamed to even show his face; the children spent their adolescence catching trains to see him at various caravan locations around New South Wales. When she asked why he'd been with this other woman, he said:

'She understands intimacy. Life, to her, is more than a practical arrangement.'

Thinking of it now made Mindy's breathing small and tight. She closed her eyes and recalled the bright patch on Hiram's ear, glowing like a jewel.

On the river bank, a group of Aboriginal children darted through the spindly trees, unaffected by the ground's harsh skin of sticks and stones on their shoeless feet. Nearby, Hiram dived into the river's deepest place and swam with strong, bold strokes to the bottom. The pressure mounted during his descent, kneading him with delicious, cold knuckles. He grasped handfuls of stones from the river's floor. Rising through the water, he imagined delivering the stones to those capering children, guiding their hands over their river-washed smoothness, showing them how they were gifts, both symbolic and tangible aspects of something ancient and enduring; but they probably knew more about it than he did. Opening his eyes, he felt the force of cold water against the membranes and lost himself in the opaque, glittering brown.

He rested under a thin shelf of rock. He should be happy; yesterday he was offered a show, a Hiram MacLeish Retrospective (was he that old?) at the Dubbo Art Gallery. The new curator, a Sydney fine arts graduate with beetroot hair, had tracked him down. Liesel Shrubber, she said her name was, flashing him her business card. She'd wanted to billet him as an Indigenous artist and seemed surprised when he protested.

'But your art, it's about the spirit of the land. It's about country,' she said. She was twenty-six, full of the vigour and clarity of her own way of seeing things. She had her hands on her hips.

'I don't want a label. I'm just myself,' he said quietly.

Inwardly he'd felt a surprising anger towards her, and he pressed his lips together to avoid saying any more. It was triggered by Liesel's knowing use of the word *country*. Why did she have this language, this trendy artspeak that she flipped around so impudently, when it was in his blood, in his bones, in the shape of his face, in the breath of his ancestors, and he *couldn't even let himself own it?*

The irony of assisting Jeffrey Winterson choose flowers for Nadia was not lost on Mindy. Here he was, all cleft chin, long legs and salt-and-pepper eyelashes, Kouros supplanting the fragrant air of her shop for the first time, asking Mindy to pick out flowers for an old rival she'd introduced him to! She rejected her initial impulse to suggest carnations, gathering instead a lively bouquet of kangaroo-paw in red tissue.

'You've got a good eye, Mindy,' said Jeffrey appreciatively, flicking open his wallet. 'And you're looking lovely today, as usual.'

'Oh really?' she said. How eager her voice sounded. She picked out a card from the stand on the counter. 'And a card to go with the flowers, Jeffrey? It's on the house,' she said.

Jeffrey grinned. 'Gee, thanks Mindy. Never thought I'd be doing this again. Got to hand it to the Singles Club. Thought it'd be embarrassing, but well…' He tucked the velvety flowers under his arm. 'Look at me now!'

Mindy had married because she thought she had to when she fell pregnant. She was barely eighteen when Francis De Cruze, so good looking, so *touchable* with his velvety black curls, had coaxed her to the river bank where he imagined no one would see them. It was the summer before Hiram MacLeish left for the Northern Territory, and he was spending it with his mother. Most Yanco students would go to university and get degrees in farm management, or take over the family business, but Hiram was planning freedom from academic and familial ties in the form of a job. Mindy somehow knew this without being told. She'd occasionally caught sight of Hiram by the river, walking, reading, sketching, or simply lying on the ground and staring at the sky. She'd often idly wondered if he was witness to Francis's expert kisses, to the seduction that so altered the course of her own future.

What Francis had said about understanding intimacy wounded her — far more than he would have supposed. How dare he criticise her lack of intimacy or whatever he called it when they married on the basis of a roll by the river bank? What did he expect? He had stolen the life she might have had.

Hiram was sketching grass with charcoal, just idle doodles, when the phone rang. There was a cool breeze coming through the windows, the sky was full of opalescent clouds, it smelt of rain. He picked up the phone, smudging the plastic surface.

'Hi there, is that Hiram? It's Mindy De Cruze,' came the woman's uncompromising voice. Hiram nudged the receiver between his ear and shoulder and wiped his hands on his jeans, as though she stood before him and could see his chalky fingers.

'I was at your exhibition the other day, Hiram. The Retrospective. I had no idea.'

Hiram found himself swallowing hard, an unusual, airy sort of feeling unfolding in his chest. He waited for her to continue.

'The thing is, Hiram, I don't really know anything about art. I never went to university or anything. Look, I know this might seem like a presumption – but I wondered if you'd talk about it with me?'

It was after reading the editor's puzzled review of Hiram's exhibition in the *Mail* that Mindy went to have a look for herself. She saw why the editor – a quick fellow, but not sophisticated – was perplexed.

She stood among the artworks not knowing where to start. She walked towards Number 1, read the title and stared at the sculpture. It was utterly foreign. She went on to the next work, standing before it like a pilgrim, penitent and respectful of its wholeness, as though the art would somehow deliver its meaning to her. But it didn't, and the longer she stood there, the more she felt excluded from this world.

Mindy rested on a bench, twitching with frustration. She had come wanting to understand. To her left was an artwork mounted on a waist-high pillar; it was a piece of wildly curling Mallee root, polished to a high gloss and speared with a large shard of Perspex. It was called *Arrival*. In front of her was a vast blue canvas with a loop of trees and figures at the bottom. Mindy recognised the river bank and saw the figures were three children, their bodies thin and lithe and dark against the boiling sapphire hotpot of the sky.

After several hours she had thoroughly explored the rocky outcrops of Hiram's inner landscape. Although its secrets remained undisclosed, she was aware of a subtle change in her body, an unwinding, something which permitted her to leave.

Maybe things were beginning for him, thought Hiram, opening the door of the ute in the steaming car park. He felt possessed of an idiotic excitement which made him grin manically, and when he tried to control his lips the smile kept bursting through like a bed spring. Great drops of rain sizzled on the asphalt. Mindy was already heading towards him, light-footed, almost skipping.

'Isn't this great, after all the heat?' she shouted over the din of the downpour, her hands gesturing to the sky.

'Yes, it's great,' he shouted back.

As she came up alongside him, Mindy put her hand in the crook of Hiram's arm and together they walked like old friends towards the art gallery's double doors.

Later, Mindy made him coffee in her pretty pinewood kitchen while he sat on a stool at the bench, sniffing hungrily at the spiced fruit loaf as it came out of the oven. Gleaming saucepans and utensils hung from hooks overhead, and dust-free shelves housed ceramic canisters labelled *flour*, *sugar* and *salt*.

Through her kitchen window, Hiram saw the tall and curly-haired sons working on a car in the driveway in the shade of Mindy's jacaranda tree. The rain clouds had vanished, leaving a sky so blue the jacaranda blossoms seemed to dissolve into it. Hiram felt grizzled and rough in this girlish kitchen and yet he didn't mind. He was enjoying the unfamiliar experience of homely food being prepared for him, and witnessing Mindy's domestic orderliness. It reminded him of how she was at the Singles Club, restrained yet generous, quietly nurturing without wanting gratitude.

Mindy served the fruit loaf slathered with melting butter and poured coffee into a pink cup resting on a saucer, offered milk in a small pink jug. She sat opposite Hiram, pouring her own coffee – no milk, no sugar – in her careful, proper way, and he could have laughed at the contrast between this controlled woman in her kitchen and the way she'd looked in the car park, practically running towards him, umbrella-less, her soaking shirt revealing ribs and breasts and collarbone, full of glee at the rain. There were other ways of being free, Hiram thought, that he could show her.

'What are you grinning at, Hiram MacLeish?' Mindy asked, smiling as though she guessed.

'Something I haven't thought of before,' he said.

'Such as?'

'Well,' he said. 'I *really* don't want to go back to the Singles Club.'

The mention of the Singles Club started them laughing so heartily that it took some minutes before they noticed Jason and Tony in the kitchen staring; a pair of grease-stained, gawping giants, bamboozled at the spectacle of their mother's mirth. Another bright peal of laughter erupted from Mindy at the sight of their dumbfounded faces. Hiram stood up and shook their hands.

'What have you done to Mum?' demanded Jason. 'She looks like she's gone round the twist.'

'So what? It's about time!' said Mindy tipsily. 'But Hiram, don't go,' she added, as he drained the pink cup and picked up his Akubra from the counter. He was made shy by those oafish sons of hers. She cast them a cross look and followed Hiram to the verandah where they said goodbye, and he bent to kiss her on the cheek. Then she watched as he walked down her driveway, past the boys' wrecked car and climbed into the ute parked by the nature strip.

Back in the kitchen, the boys were waiting, ready to burst into teasing, their whole bodies in attitudes of unspoken impudence. Mindy didn't care. She felt like singing. Her face was warm with the memory of Hiram's kiss, the rasp of his cool cheek, the tiny scratch of new whiskers that no one else could hear, full of promise.

ALL YOUR MOTHERS

AT THE NEW HOUSE THE BED IS SMALL and tightly tucked with a sheet and a knitted blanket, and it smells of pickles. At Mrs Wilson's, I had a doona printed with sail boats but no pets. Here at Mrs Gloucester's there's a cat. Even though the bed is neat and tight the cat's still allowed to sleep on it, with me. Sometimes during the night she pushes my chest with her paws, like she's making me into a nest. Her name is Farmer. That's a strange name for a cat, I tell Mrs Gloucester.

Another boy named her that because he wanted to be a farmer, says Mrs Gloucester. She tucks me into my pickle bed each night and sings me a lullaby. One time when I felt sick at school she came and carried me to the car.

Cling on to my hip, she told me. So I did, and I put my head against her shoulder like I've seen babies do and pretended I was her little boy.

We go to church. I've been to church with other foster mothers and fathers but this one has nice ceilings and a playground where we go after Sunday School, and the mothers come outside and give us cookies, not shop biscuits but cookies baked in ovens with sultanas in them, and oats. I choose the ones I saw Mrs Gloucester bake. They are fat and golden.

All the children play on the swings or climb the rope ladders except for one little girl standing next to me. The teacher said you have no mummy, she says, gazing at me with eyes as soft as water.

I say, I do have a mummy but I don't know where she is.

That's even worse, says the girl. My name is Tessa Carter.

Even though she's not as big as me, Tessa takes my hand. Hers is cool and white.

My name is Ashley, I say. I take my hand away, but not so fast it hurts her feelings. I don't want the other children to see me holding hands. Her cool hand leaves mine warm.

When I grow up I could marry Tessa Carter.

I like Mrs Gloucester very much. But then she gets sick and has to go to hospital, and the lady with the clipboard comes and takes me to Mrs Boots's house.

At Mrs Boots's I share a bunk with another boy called Bobby. Because he was there first he gets the top bunk. The sheets are soft, with tiny bumps on them – they're old and they get washed a lot, nearly every day. They have a fluffy dog at Mrs Boots's but he has to sleep outside. Once I let him inside and he pooed in the bedroom, and Mrs Boots shouted at me. She brought in a bucket of boiling water and a bottle of eucalyptus oil, and I couldn't go to sleep that night because the fumes made my eyes sting. The poor dog got walloped. My ears were full of whimpers while I rubbed my eyes with the bumpy sheets, and I wished Farmer was with me, with her loud purring and bright stare.

After Mrs Boots's, I go to Mrs Cook's. She jokes with me about her name – she really can't cook. Mr Cook does the cooking. He makes sausages and mash and baked beans, but if he's late home from work me and Mrs Cook eat cereal – sometimes she slices bananas on top. To make it more healthy for you, she says.

After Mrs Cook, it's Mr and Mrs Gordon in a house with brown carpet that always smells of garlic because they love spaghetti and meat sauce. Mr Gordon is much older than Mrs

Gordon, with pinkish kind of skin and a white beard. He has a soft body, too, and wears T-shirts instead of work shirts – he doesn't go to work that much because he's scared of going outside. *I'm not telling lies*, he tells me, *if I go out too much the blood cuts off from my head and I faint.*

He's always there when I get home from school. They have a dog, a long-haired Daschund called Frankie. Mr Gordon trims him so he doesn't leave long hairs on the couch. He pushes all of Frankie's fur one way with a long-toothed comb and cuts it short with barber's scissors. He gives Frankie Eskimo Pies from the freezer and sometimes he gives me one, especially if I have a cuddle.

At first I like Mr Gordon, but he always wants to hold me on his knee and I'm too big for that. He keeps rude pictures in an envelope, and he's showing me one day when Mrs Gordon comes home early from shopping. She rushes at me and pulls me off his knee, ripping up the photos and saying, *I'm sorry, I'm sorry*. She puts her arms around me and sort of cries down my neck. I keep saying I'm okay, but she doesn't believe me. Or maybe she's not listening.

I ask the lady with the clipboard if there's any chance I could go back to Mrs Gloucester but she's very sorry to tell me that Mrs Gloucester died. After that there's a cold box, a brick of ice that sits in between my ribs and my tummy.

Sometimes at night I try to warm it by holding my hands on it and then hotness comes up my throat and makes me want to cry. The cold box comes with me wherever I go. It's there when I meet my mother.

My mother lives in a shared house with other women – I think there are doctors there somewhere, too. The lady with the clipboard takes me to a little room with two green couches, and a brown coffee table with an ashtray made of shiny red glass. An unwashed window looks out onto a concrete yard.

My mother's not even as big as I am. She's very thin. Her hair is sort of grey-blonde. She's wearing a long-sleeved shirt, and the sleeves are see-through; I can see the scabs on her arms. I know what they are because I'm nearly a teenager by now.

She smiles at me and says, I'm getting better, Ashley. Every day I'm getting a bit better. And then you'll be able to come home to me. Not here, but a real home.

She doesn't have enough teeth. But I smile back and say, Yes, that will be good. I'm betraying her by smiling and acting like I want to be with her when in my heart I'm wishing she was Mrs Gloucester.

By the time I get to Mrs Andrew's they say I'm too wild. But what can they expect when I've got a dying junkie for a mother, no father and no home of my own? I got kicked out of my last school for selling dope to my mates.

Mrs Andrew isn't a Christian, she's a Buddhist, and she's typed out the Eightfold Path and tacked it to the wall in my bedroom. She tells me that selling dope to other children doesn't fit in with Right Livelihood, which is Number Five.

She wants me to call her Deva but I call her Mrs Andrew. She's got a son who rides with bikies. His name is Eric and he drops in for curries. She makes these fish and vegetable curries, and these little noodle baskets with a fried egg at the bottom. She says they're Sri Lankan – 'Hoppers', she calls them. They're actually pretty cool but I don't say much about them, just eat them. I don't know where Mr Andrew is and I don't ask.

Eric mostly ignores me. He's got tattoos all over. On one arm he's got a bearded god, naked except for a cloak and helmet, blowing a horn that curves beside his body like a snake.

I really like your bike, I tell him one evening after he's finished his fish curry.

It's a '92 black fat-boy with solid steel rims, he says. I'll take you for a ride.

Oh Eric, says Mrs Andrew. I don't know about that.

I won't go over two-fifty, I promise, he says, straight-faced.

Keep to the speed limit, she warns, or he stays here with me.

Eric keeps his own promise. He gives me his helmet and we fly over the roads out to the freeway, me watching the speedometer needle over his shoulder in fascinated horror. We're flying. Every once in a while I look away to the trees and factories smeared like paint as the wind threshes my skin.

When I go out with my mates I don't drink beer but whisky: it scalds my throat and melts the ice brick. There's a really pretty girl called Tracy who has a lot of parties and her own car, and I get into trouble with her because she's a bitch. One night, I'm standing near her, drunkenly turning meat on the barbecue, when I hear her say to her friend that I'm fucked in the head because I'm a foster kid. Her friend nudges her too late, and I storm through the house, down the front steps and into the garden, where her dad's left gardening shears by the letterbox. Whisky is boiling in my gullet and red lights are popping in the corners of my eyes. I grab hold of the letterbox so hard that splinters wedge into my fingernails.

Hey Ash.

I turn around to see Tracy jigging from side to side in her white T-shirt and shorts. The action makes her brown kneecaps go up and down like yoyos.

Don't go, Ash. You can't help the way you are.

Oh yeah? How am I?

You know. A bit fucked-up. Everyone says so.

An image of the ice brick flashes into my mind, only it's no longer a brick but a railway sleeper that's caught fire. I can barely control the fierce shaking in my body. I lean over and pick up the gardening shears. She watches me.

What are you doing? Put them down, Ash.

I like hearing the fear in her voice. I don't put the shears down but brandish them in front of me. Their awkward weight makes them fall forward and the tip grazes my foot, drawing blood.

Searing red light pours out of my temples. Walking over to her car – the one her dad bought her – I raise the shears and smash them down on the trunk. A gash opens in the shiny metal, and then I shatter each headlight. I drop the shears and run all the way to Mrs Andrew's.

Eric's bike is parked out the front, under the massive spruce tree. At the front door, I hear the telephone ring. It's got to be Tracy's dad – or maybe the cops. Eric's keys are on the dresser, so I grab them and go, my foot dripping blood in the hallway and on the porch.

The motorbike's leather seat is cool from the spruce's shadow. I pull the helmet roughly over my head and snap on the strap. The key turns, the motor snarls, the road sings its hot, dark-blue song. The wheels kick over the kerb and behind me on the porch is Eric, shouting *STOP*, but there's no time to stop now. I have to hold it, just hold all this power together, just get this bike straight, just get it to behave right and stop lurching. The bike's too strong. I don't know how to make it stop veering horribly to the left, towards that brick fence, and in the end I accelerate instead of braking and the bike bucks over the kerb and ploughs towards the bricks, taking me with it.

Mrs Andrew says that when I was barely conscious in the intensive care unit I said one word. *Tessa*.

It's strange I said Tessa; my dreams are of Mrs Gloucester and the tightly tucked bed with the knitted blanket, and Farmer's paws kneading my chest. When I wake, the smell of pickles becomes the smell of saline solution. Mrs Andrew is beside me, with an Indian scarf pulled tight over her light hair.

There's no girl at your school called Tessa, she says, reproachfully. You've got to stop being so wild, Ashley, or they'll take you away from me and put you in the boys' home.

My body feels numb and airless. Something is binding my head and jaw together. From the corner of my left eye I just see the shadow of it, a wire claw.

Don't try to talk now, she says. She sandwiches my hand between her warm palms and there's a wet glint in her eyes.

It's weeks before I'm back at Mrs Andrew's house and we still have daily appointments with the physiotherapist. I don't want to spend so much time in bed but I have to because I'm so tired; sometimes I sleep all day. Sleep comes up to me in a new way, like the road did that evening, petrol blue and glistening with smeared, dirty rainbows. One afternoon I wake up and Eric's sitting at the end of my bed, smoking. He's got a new tattoo on his skull.

Sorry about the bike, I mumble.

Yeah, the Harley's fucked, mate.

I'll pay you back.

Eric looks at me sideways. Will you? He scratches his chin. I don't get it, he says. You've got everything you need.

I have no mother, I say, but wish I hadn't.

Be grateful for all your mothers, he says. You got all the mothering you need.

I don't have a father.

Neither do I, mate, but do you see that holding me back? And you know what? You're very lucky that you came to Deva last.

I realise then that Eric is not Mrs Andrew's flesh and blood son but a foster kid like me. I want to keep talking with him but I don't know how. Behind his head is the Eightfold Path on that dog-eared paper. He finishes his cigarette.

Pay back Tracy's dad before you pay me back, he says, getting up.

I want him to stay – even a minute longer is something – so I say, What does that tattoo mean? The one of the man with the – is it a horn?

Yeah, that's a horn. That's Heimdall.

Heimdall?

Don't you know anything? Heimdall's a Norse god. He had nine mothers.

And suddenly Eric's stony face breaks into a self-aware grin, which I've never seen before and I stare at it, drinking it up.

Is that who you're like?

The grin disappears. Nah mate, I'm a long way off that. Heimdall guards the gods. He knows who can come into Asgard, and who can't.

Did Mrs Andrew tell you about him?

No, he says. Another one did. And you should call her Deva. It's the least you can do.

Now I'm a man and can find out things for myself. When I find Tessa Carter, she's standing in the same playground where I met her, sipping tea and talking to the old ladies. On the table beside me there's a platter of cookies. I take one and wait for her to see me, watching the children swing from the rope ladders. I've always hoarded my memories without retracing my steps, so today's a new experience. Seeing that playground makes the dry cookies hard to swallow.

Mid-conversation, Tessa looks across to me. Her eyes squint with recognition. Her astonished face thrills me.

I've forgotten your name, she says when she comes over, but I remember you.

She's lived in one place all these years. She works with autistic students at the local school. As we talk I sense her quietness and how she keeps thoughts hidden from view like humps in a river. I say, Do you remember you held my hand?

Of course I do. I remember you standing there bravely – not having your own mother seemed like the worst thing in the world. You came a few times and then you were gone. When I heard your foster mother had died I knew you wouldn't come back, and I imagined you going to live in a stranger's house.

I'm not sentimental but when Tessa tells me this I feel myself sucked backwards from my life, as if seeing something working in it from far away, like ripples in a pond spreading outwards and returning. Boldly, I take her cool white hand. She laughs and says I'm crazy but I'm not crazy any more. Right actions lead to sound states of mind.

I release Tessa's hand. She walks with me to the shaded avenue of oak trees where the Harley's parked. Behind us, the gate creaks closed on the children climbing and swinging in their sunlit playground. In front of us the road lengthens over a hill and meets the sky.

LOVEST THOU ME

Yasmin noticed James's dressing-gown in the spare room closet when she went to grab her running shoes.

She put her face against the soft cloth and breathed it in: only the faintest trace of him was still there. In life he had been like a father to her. Now she found herself thinking of him as tenderly as a son. She felt something in one of the pockets and drew out the little blue book. He'd told her he found it 'heavy going' and couldn't finish reading it. Yasmin saw that he'd turned down a corner, on page twenty-five. She read the entry marked *August 18, 1915*, and wept.

On the golf course Yasmin chased the dog. She stopped and spun around, feeling the old childish terror of getting lost, searching for the orange flag she had passed and the bridge she had crossed. The golf course eerily shuffled back into and out of itself, like an accordion. Gums and pines unfolded with changed colours, the greens undulated in every direction, the houses at the boundaries melded with shadows. She was lost – and the sun was falling fast. She clicked her tongue, angry for going too far. What if Romney woke up and disturbed David or Marion? She shouldn't have left them.

'Tug. *Tug*! Come back here, you bad boy!'

The dog stopped under a pine tree. Joy dissolved from his limbs and he reverted to the posture he'd taken since James's death. He drooped his head and hunched his shoulders. It wasn't his beloved master's booming Yorkshire voice calling him to heel, it was that interloper, the daughter-in-law, a daft waft of a woman who doesn't know where she is going.

It was only six weeks since Marion had come home from the palliative care unit where James was dying. She sat mutely on the couch while Yasmin fussed over her, bringing first a cup of tea, then a bowl of broccoli soup and chunks of bread.

'Want to play dominoes, Gram?' asked Romney.

'Not now,' said Yasmin, more sharply than she meant. He puckered his lower lip, but thankfully he didn't cry.

Her mother-in-law's eyes were glazed with exhaustion. She ate the soup too quickly and dabbed at the green splashed on her trousers, breathing heavily.

'David was so good,' she said. 'James was saying *let me die* over and over. David stroked his hand and said, *It's coming, Dad. It's coming.*'

Marion pressed her fingertips to her temples briefly and looked through the window to the backyard. Romney, who had lined up all the dominoes and had a fingertip poised, was listening.

'The trees need water,' Marion muttered.

'I'll do it,' said Yasmin.

'No,' said Marion. 'I'd like to.' But she didn't get up. 'They've made a camp bed for David,' she went on, quietly, 'so he can stay each night. I suppose I should stay with him really. Oh Yasmin, how long do you think he can go *on* like this?'

That evening, when Yasmin read *Scuffy the Tugboat* to Romney and tucked him into bed, he said: 'I don't like it when Scuffy gets to the ocean.'

'But he gets saved, doesn't he?' said Yasmin. 'The daddy and the little boy find him and take him home.'

'It's scary.'

'That's what makes the story exciting.'

'I don't like exciting.'

'But every time we read it, they find Scuffy and keep him safe.'

David first brought her to meet his parents James and Marion when she was nineteen, shy and hopeful, full of inarticulate thoughts and feelings. They drove up to the new house standing by the golf course. The house – white and sharp, shade cloth pegged out at various angles to protect the western windows – reminded her of a yacht. That evening, its clean outline had been softened by the mango cheeks of sunset.

Yasmin yanked at her shirt nervously.

'Relax. They're great,' David said, turning off the engine. 'Make sure you speak up. Dad likes people who have something to say for themselves.'

A prickle of sweat broke out on the back of Yasmin's neck. *Speak up?* What on earth could she possibly say?

She followed David down the broad driveway. Yasmin expected a modern interior to match the outside. Instead, she found cosy floral sofas, whitewashed wood and china ornaments. David's father strolled towards them, smiling.

'Na'then,' he bellowed.

Dinner was Marion's speciality: a roast with rich gravy, mushy peas and crisp Yorkshire puddings. Yasmin found herself blundering, tongue-tied, as she struggled to follow James's conversation. He shared David's cutting humour, but broke up sentences and put things in a different order, and said it all in an accent so broad that sometimes she scarcely caught his meaning. She nodded and smiled, hoping he wouldn't find her slow on the uptake.

'David says you go to church,' James said, pushing his carrots to one side of the plate. 'Why do you do that?'

'Well,' Yasmin said. 'I believe in God.' How gauche that sounded. Under the table, her toes clenched in her boots.

James shook his head. 'Say it again!' he boomed. He was only sixty but already hard of hearing.

'I believe in Christ,' she said loudly, her skin burning all the way from her hairline to her collarbone. David was grinning at her from across the table, one eyebrow raised. So? Hadn't he *told* her to speak up?

'I think that's good,' James said, unexpectedly. 'I can't go to church. I can't believe in it. But it's a good thing to believe in.'

That first mention of God was the beginning of a conversation that went on for almost two decades. On the darkening golf course, Yasmin wondered if it had served James at all. It seemed unfinished.

The hills rose and sank as she walked, amorphous as ocean waves. This would never happen if she was with James. He would find his way back easily. He'd never get lost in the first place. Yasmin chose someone's back fence and began to walk alongside it.

'Keep to the edges. Eventually you'll find the house,' she told herself.

The twilit grass was blue and velvety. Tug seemed to have vanished altogether. Despite the heat, the air was fresh and humming with bird calls, and if Yasmin wasn't worrying about Tug and getting home she would be enjoying herself. She didn't want Romney waking David, who was suffering mysterious pains in the gut; or Marion, so newly widowed and needing rest.

Yasmin's thighs ached. There was a hot wedge of pain under each shoulderblade, probably from sleeping on the couch so poor David could thrash about freely in the double bed. All of them struggled to sleep in the stifling summer air. Although Marion ran the air conditioners with a devil-may-care desperation, none of them could escape an atmosphere turgid with exhaustion and absence. Bereavement was not what Yasmin had anticipated. It was an untried kind of sadness, pervasive and circuitous, hanging around like smoke. Without warning it would reach inside and give her heart a shocking squeeze, enough to make her gasp.

'Tug! *Tug!*' she yelled into the shadows. She ran into a silvery clump of trees, thinking she glimpsed the dog's silhouette. On she ran to the next group of trees and the next before halting, out of breath, her hands on her knees. Underfoot dead pine needles made a fragrant nest.

'Tug. Where *are* you? Please!' she cried.

Peering through a tangle of creepers climbing a nearby fence, she saw a canoe in someone's backyard with its oar left next to it, pale and empty under the moon. She stood very still, hoping to hear the dog's pant as he approached. But nothing – except kookaburras breaking into a cacophony nearby.

'Stupid dog,' she said.

It was impossible not to like James. He hid nothing. His moods sat on his face openly: disgust, joy, boredom. He said what he thought, regardless of the beliefs or sensitivities of his listeners. In the presence of someone he liked he became incandescent, as though a candle glowed behind his bones.

Once when Romney was a baby, she'd taken him into the living room for his morning feed and found James striding up and down in front of a dark television set.

'I got up early to watch the rugby,' he grumbled, 'and there's a bloody power cut.'

He dropped into an armchair. His lower lip pushed into his upper lip and his mouth curved down like a horseshoe.

'Go back to bed,' suggested Yasmin, who was so tired from mothering that she couldn't believe anyone would be up when they didn't have to be.

James didn't answer. When the lights came on he didn't bother turning on the television. Yasmin fed the baby quietly, not venturing to speak again. At dawn, red parrots flew down to the empty feeder and squawked at the window, stirring James from his melancholy reverie.

'Look at that! The power's back and I didn't even notice.'

'It's been on half an hour.'

'Really?' said James.

'You were too busy enjoying being miserable.'

For an awkward minute Yasmin thought she'd said the wrong thing. But then James nodded, a broad smile of self-recognition transforming his features.

'Ha!' he said. 'You're absolutely right.'

Soon after, they began their evening walks on the golf course with Tug. James liked to talk, Yasmin liked to listen. She revelled in the richness of his voice, his easy shuffling of sentences, his jokes that – even after years – still took her a few minutes to get. She would search his deadpan face and find the twinkle in his eye, and laugh.

'Do you believe in God because you're afraid of hell?' James once asked her, as they set out at a cracking pace under a glowing lilac dusk.

'Oh no,' Yasmin had replied.

'What makes you believe?'

'I just always did; I never found a compelling argument that stopped me feeling that it was true,' she said. 'But I know – for you, for many people – that's not good enough.'

Yasmin was disturbed that her thinking seemed to liquefy and coil away from the hard question. She couldn't find words to explain how her convictions were wired into the very substance of herself. She knew she must address her mind to the question, not only her heart. Love the Lord your God with all your soul, all your heart, all your mind and all your strength; that was the instruction.

Tug, only a puppy, had bounded ahead over the greens. In the distance, a lone golfer disappeared behind a hill. The air smelled of pine needles and onions on someone's barbecue.

'In *my* opinion,' said James, 'if God was real it wouldn't be so hard to know. He'd show up at the foot of my bed and invite me to follow Him. None of this guessing, this *faith*.'

'Did you ever get around to reading that book, *Life after Life*?'

'Hmph,' he snorted. 'I've got two copies of that now. Friends keep buying it for me. People die on the operating table and go into the light. One person said the light was a loving being. Jesus, I suppose. They heard a question that seemed to come from the light.'

'What question?' she asked.

'Lovest thou me?'

Yasmin stopped walking for the briefest second and took a breath. *Lovest thou me* chimed in her like a faraway bell. Hiding her eagerness she said, 'What did you think about that?'

'Can't trust it,' said James, shaking his head. 'What if the brain has a trick where you see light when you almost die? What if something you heard at school comes back as a memory? Nothing can prove it to my brain. Or yours.'

They strode in silence all the way to where the lip of the course met the market gardens. Sprinklers sprayed hard silver beads over the deep green cabbagey sprouts rising from dark furrows. She and James paused and watched what was growing before turning back. As usual, Yasmin couldn't remember which direction was home; she followed James while he whistled 'The Grand Old Duke of York'. The setting sun returned the red colour of his youth to his muted hair.

David didn't sleep much during James's final week. He supervised the electronic drivers delivering morphine into his father's cancer-wracked body. Sometimes the pain would overtake the morphine, and James would mutter *oh dear, oh dear, oh dear*, and moan pitifully. David patted his father's forehead with a damp cloth. He watched as James sat in bed, tearing tissues apart with his fingers and holding his hand out for another, until the sheet was covered with tissues. He stitched the air with an unseen needle held between his forefinger and thumb.

'What's he doing?' David whispered to the nurse when she came to check on him.

'Oh – they call it plucking,' she replied. 'He's confused.'

But to David there was nothing confused about the precision of his father's gestures. When the nurse left, he leaned forward and asked his father.

'I'm making cloaks,' James replied. 'One for me and one for Romney.'

Early the next morning, James seemed to be placing invisible objects in a row across the bed cover.

'What are you doing, Dad?' David asked softly, intrigued.

'Playing dominoes,' said James.

When David repeated this to Yasmin, he couldn't keep the emotion from his voice. 'There was something so innocent about it. There he was, every inch a man of the world. And he was *playing dominoes*.'

When Yasmin first learned how sick James was, fear had lurched through her like a train. Now, alone on the golf course, she sat cross-legged on the grass, feeling rigid: a rod of grief held her upright while her edges grew spongy. A milk-mist moon was rising in the east. Three quarters of the sky was turquoise, and to the west it was stained mulberry. The colours were soft yet intense, like chalk worked so deeply into paper it had lost its powdery quality and fused with the surface.

Staring into this sky, Yasmin found a piece of herself dislodging, flying out to meet James, praying for him with a desperate, yearning hopefulness. There was a round hardness jammed in her throat like the end of a broom handle. The prayers were promises. Declarations of love. The frantic nature of them reminded her of the one time James had prayed.

'When David was a baby we almost lost him,' he'd told her. 'I went into the men's room and got onto my knees. I was wringing my hands and praying to a God I didn't believe in to save my baby's life. Over and over again. Please God, let him live. *Please God.*'

James had surgery, and chemotherapy peeled the rosiness from him. Most of the time he was too sick to talk. It was happening; he was dying. Yasmin saw it each time she looked at him.

She craved their old conversation about life after death; she didn't care how hard the question was, she'd strive harder than ever for a satisfactory answer. But James had lost interest. If she sat beside him on the couch he would lift her hand to kiss it, and talk of politics or his grandchild. There was no spark of the old debate. And somehow it seemed bad taste to talk about dying with someone who *was* dying.

'Why do you want to talk to him about it so much?' asked David. 'Maybe he's come to terms with things on his own.'

'He doesn't know what to expect,' said Yasmin. 'I've read that if you don't know where you are, you get imprisoned by your own perceptions. You get lost.'

As soon as the words were out of her mouth, she was suspicious of her own evangelical fervour. And yet if she tried to dampen it down it sprang back up in her with renewed urgency. The next time they went to visit she handed James a slim blue volume: the book of communications from the dead soldier.

'Yasmin's given me a book,' James said to Marion.

'How nice,' said Marion, her habitual brightness of manner contrasting with the dark circles around her eyes. She was worn out with tending to him.

Yasmin said, hurriedly: 'It's just if you want to, you know, read something. I liked it.'

After almost twenty years, she sounded as gauche as ever.

Trudging by the fences, Yasmin caught sight of the bridge. Ah! Excellent. Now she was getting somewhere. She released the cyclone wire and ran towards the rickety wooden bridge. As she ran, Tug emerged from the shadows, springing behind her.

'There you are!' she cried.

The wooden railing felt dry and strange – it alarmed her. The bridge she'd crossed earlier was metal, not wood. She remembered a cool cylinder under her palm. Or was that someone's back fence? She couldn't remember. This *always* happened. She memorised the order of things, their touch, feel and location, and then they got jumbled.

'Just cross the bridge and go home,' she told herself. 'Go on, Tug. Lead the way. Sniff your way home.' The terrier lay down on the ground, his tongue hanging sideways out of his mouth. 'So much for trusting the animal instinct,' she murmured.

Yasmin clipped the leash onto his collar and pulled him over the bridge. She spoke loudly into the night: 'If I'm going back home, I turn right, don't I? No, you idiot, it's left!' Then she laughed and said, 'Just keep turning left. Isn't that how you get out of a maze, Tug? Keep turning left?'

Ahead, she saw a blaze of houselights twinkling at the boundaries of the dark and she rushed forward, her feet bouncing on the trim grass.

On the night of his father's death, David felt its approach. The atmosphere in the death room was not unlike that of a birth room: a space between worlds. Something was vast and wide open, with the force of a gale yet utterly still.

David swept the scrunched-up tissues and little plastic cups used for cordial or ice into the bin. He poured fresh water into the vase holding a red rose that Romney had brought from Marion's garden. He hung up his father's dressing-gown and pushed the slippers under the bed and carried a stack of *Herald Suns* out to the waiting room. He took the bin out. Then, standing a respectful distance from the bed, he raised his arms and bowed his head.

Yasmin imagined James leaving his body, rising above the bed, looking down at the son praying with his arms outstretched like a priest; seeing the clean surfaces and everything white save that fragrant red rose, a heavenly thing, a lantern of carmine light to carry him over.

Tug strained at the lead, almost pulling her arm out of its socket. The lights were not coming from Marion's as she'd hoped. It was the golf club house.

'They'll have a phone I can use, surely,' she said to herself.

She climbed over the back fence and made her way through the gardens. Behind dozens of glass doors were diners, mature women in floral dresses with their husbands in collared shirts, drinking champagne, beer or wine. Wearing old shorts, a singlet and runners, Yasmin knew she looked wild and sweaty from running in the dark.

She tied Tug to a column and walked inside, blushing at the stares she attracted. She walked up to the counter.

'Hi,' she said to the surprised barman. 'This is embarrassing but I got lost on the golf course and I need to use the phone.'

Marion answered immediately. 'Yasmin! Where on earth are you?'

Yasmin explained, and said she would be home soon, in a taxi.

'Nonsense,' said Marion, in the tone that brooked no argument. 'Wait there. I'll come and get you.'

Yasmin walked out through the foyer of etched glass, refracting bright splinters of red, blue and green from the brash Christmas lights. She collected Tug and hauled him to the driveway. She sat on the kerb and waited, stroking the dog's neck. The night air seemed warmer than her own breath. The phrase she'd read earlier floated through her thoughts. *I can come so near to you, I can feel you bodily...* It was the dead soldier's message to his sister. *I can squeeze your hand but you cannot feel it.*

The car drove up, sleek and quiet, headlights burning. Blinking, she scrambled to her feet and dragged the dog around to the passenger door. Marion smiled as she hopped in, and Yasmin was relieved to see that she hadn't troubled herself by changing – she wore a flowing cotton robe over her nightie. Light edged her pale hair.

'I can drive,' said Yasmin, embarrassed at having dragged her recuperating mother-in-law out of bed.

'No, I don't think so,' said Marion, and they both laughed. '*I* know where I'm going!'

At home, Yasmin found Romney and David sleeping peacefully. David's face looked less pale and clammy than in recent days. He was recovering.

Yasmin kicked off her runners in the closet and stroked the cuff of the dressing-gown. In the living room, she turned off the air conditioner and opened the sliding door. A warm breeze carried in the sounds of a neighbour's party, the kookaburras and singing cicadas. When she cuddled down on the sofa, she glanced across to James's photo above the television set and said goodnight to him, before reaching over and turning off the light.

SILVER HANDS: A NOVELLA

HANDS, MUSCLES, FINGERS, SKIN. Arms, elbows, blood and bone. Cooking, washing, sewing, cleaning. Lifting children, wet clothes, groceries. Sculpting clay, kneading bread.

When the pain in my arms and hands begins – a delicate ache – I don't pay it much attention, expecting it to pass. I stop lifting the children, I use the dryer instead of hauling wet laundry to the line. It's raining, anyway. The children sit on the porch and watch rain flying through layers of blue like seed pearls.

Today I'm taking Opal and Joseph to the penguins – even though Tom's left us, we can still have a nice family outing. The world has not come to an end.

What I need more than anything is a friend, so I call Paisley, who has a sympathetic ear, no husband and a three-year-old named Walter. I pack sandwiches, cake, apples and a plastic tub with peeled carrots, bottles of water, baby wipes, changes of clothes. It's a windy spring day; we bring the parkas and the children's new sheepskin mittens. We strap Walter and Opal into baby seats, squash Joseph between them and drive. It takes two hours to get to Phillip Island. *So what?* I say bullishly to Paisley. *We don't have anything better to do.*

We know the penguins are due to parade across the beach after six o'clock. We arrive at five-thirty and try to keep the children occupied as the wind thrashes under a sky of steel. Everyone's cheeks are over-pink; Walter's nose is running and he keeps wiping it on his coat sleeve. Joseph refuses to wear the hood on his parka and inexplicably empties the contents of his backpack into a rubbish bin. Paisley has brought supermarket mandarins tasting of rubber; Opal spits hers out and I look away, embarrassed.

To my surprise, Paisley doesn't ask me why Tom left. Not a word. In the car, we listened to the soundtrack of *Once* – even though I said I'd rather the little ones sang their own songs. Now Paisley's sitting on a bench as quiet as a goddess, graceful even in her parka and tracksuit pants. You can't help but look at her. Pale skin, black hair. Classic proportions. In summer she spurns bright colours and suntans, and wears white bikinis and black leather bangles to the beach.

Tom likes to say that what Paisley gains through style she loses in her lack of sensuality. 'She's pretty but kind of mannish,' he once said. There's something competitive between the two of them that I don't quite understand. How impressed Tom was when Paisley knew that his name for me – his little 'cow herding girl from Gokul' – was from an obscure poet called Mirabai.

Paisley has always been generous with me – opening herself to my wild winds – though there are some things I haven't disclosed and never will. But where is her sympathy now, when I need it so much? I stand awkwardly at the end of the crowded bench and look out at the water.

'Are you all right?' I say.

'Fine,' she says. She gives a stretched sort of smile. 'Why?'

'You seem a bit quiet.'

Walter climbs down from the platform and runs towards the sea. A soaked child is the last thing anyone wants, and Paisley goes after him. Joseph's talking to a park ranger. Opal wants to take her gumboots off and paddle.

'Absolutely not,' I say. 'We're not allowed down there!'

Rain falls from the darkening sky. A sideways slant of vanishing sun turns the rain gold. At fourteen minutes past six, the penguins start arriving in a blare of floodlights. We've been told not to use the flash on our cameras because it damages their eyes – but some idiot does, of course. The penguins toddle and bob along in small groups, necks forward, hurrying homewards after a day of fishing for anchovies and pilchards. Penguin breasts flash pearly white in the gleam of sunset; their backs are not so much black as a rich blue. Even in my numb condition, I can appreciate their comic beauty, and their habit: day after day, year after year, these little sea birds arrive at sunset, preen their feathers, and waddle to their burrows. I lose myself in the moment.

'Time to go,' says Paisley, picking up Walter.

Reluctantly, I gather our things and look around for the kids. They're not there. Hurrying along the platform, I catch sight of them, crouching down by the fence where the penguins pass by, close enough to touch.

'Wait up, chickies,' I call.

Trudging back to the car with one hand resting on Joseph's wet curls and Opal nudged hard on my hip like a koala, giggling and nibbling cake, a streak of elation passes through me.

'Shall I drive?'

'I'd prefer to,' says Paisley.

My cold wrists throb. There's no point even trying to catch Paisley's eye because she's avoiding my gaze. The elation departs as quickly as it came, and the tension builds, interrupted only by Walter's tired whining.

Paisley drives with her neat profile towards me, never taking her eyes off the road. I sag into the seat and read the signs on the freeway, *Once* blaring again. When 'Falling Slowly' comes on, I close my eyes and surrender to thoughts of Tom; in particular, the way his face looked when we were married under a jacaranda tree. Was it really twelve years ago? Skin stippled with shade and light. When the celebrant said the words, the scar on Tom's cheek – still fresh then, and bulging – was hidden by leaf shadow, his eyes down-swept under a fringe of lashes.

Walter's cry has turned into a wail and someone's making an uncanny yapping that sets my teeth on edge. 'Who's doing that?' I ask, turning around. Three shiny faces look back at me from the dark back seat: Walter's grimy and tear-stained; Opal's round-eyed; Joseph's with a cagey smile.

'Me?' says Joseph.

'Well, stop it,' I snap. 'Why are you grinning like that?'

Abruptly, I switch off the music and launch into 'Old MacDonald'.

'...*and on that farm he had a piggy, ee–ii ee–ii oo.*'

Walter joins in, snorting like a happy piglet. Opal and Joseph clap in time. Paisley tilts her chin and she catches her lip under her eye-tooth as though to stop herself from speaking.

'Let's do a cow,' I say.

'No – no ... and on that farm he had a *penguin*,' cries Joseph, and all three make variations of that awful yapping sound, laughing madly.

At home, we scrub the children with flannels and put them into fresh pyjamas. We'd arranged for Paisley and Walter to stay the night. It doesn't feel right any more, but I don't know what to say. Paisley still won't look at me – I know she won't want to change plans. Walter's port-a-cot is wedged between the children's beds. They brush their teeth and I tell them *Goldilocks and the Three Bears*, even though Joseph tells me he's 'over it'. I wince inwardly – how can a child of five be 'over' *Goldilocks*? He's learning discontent.

I retreat to the porch with a bottle of Beaujolais and two glasses, and light a cigarette. I wrap myself in a shawl. There's not much to see out here. The front garden is dull and formless, the stars snug behind robust clouds like army blankets. Oh, for a bold moon! When there's a moon the garden comes alive in contrasting patterns. I love the silvery silhouettes and rivulets of moonlight winding like white blood, sharpening the edges of the shadows.

Paisley appears at the door. 'Should we watch a DVD?' she asks.

'Sure,' I say. I don't move.

She pulls a woolly beanie over her ears and sits beside me. We drink in silence. Paisley never smokes.

'What is it?' I say.

'What?'

'Something's bugging you.'

'I'm just tired. I'm tired of being on my own.' She pauses and says disparagingly: 'Boring.'

She never wants to talk about herself and sure enough the next question steers the conversation towards me.

'So, are you doing any work at the moment?'

'No,' I reply. 'I can't prepare the clay. You've really got to knead it and it makes my arms hurt like mad. Ruth'll be angry, but what can I do? I'm sick of doing those organic replicas, anyway.'

'You've got to do what sells. Especially now.'

What I'd really like to do is sculpt the human form. Limbs and faces. Whenever I try, the clay turns hostile and unwieldy; I haven't made a human shape for years. There's no point discussing this with Paisley. She's not very interested in what I do, but on an ordinary day I could count on her for some sympathy in dealing with my agent, Ruth, who can be a shark. After a few silent moments, I ask: 'What about you – what have you been up to?'

'Nothing much. Teaching a few violin lessons, a bit of house-cleaning.'

'Are you sure nothing else is worrying you?'

Paisley's face contracts. She's told me off about this before, my 'need to interrogate'. 'How are you coping without Tom?' she asks, instead.

This is the question I've been waiting for all day, so intense is my need to talk. 'I'm not,' I say. 'I feel like I've been hit by a train. I just didn't see it coming.'

'What does he say?'

'He doesn't know if he feels the same way about me any more. He moved out. It feels so – final.'

At the farm they've lit a fire, and soft puffs of smoke waft from their chimney over the fields towards us. I take a last drag of my cigarette and stub it into the ashtray.

'I just can't imagine bringing up the children without him.'

'Well, you won't, will you? He'll be involved.'

'It's not the same.'

Paisley's never been married; she's never even been in a long-term relationship. She knows nothing of how we've shaped our private republic. He moved out, but I'm the one who feels exiled.

'And what will happen when he hooks up with someone else?' I murmur. 'How soon does this happen?'

'Well, it will happen,' says Paisley. 'He's an attractive man.'

'But maybe not for a while. I mean, maybe women won't want to sleep with someone who's already saddled with kids.'

Even as I say this, I know it's nonsense. Paisley says: '*I* wouldn't mind.'

In the silence that follows this bombshell we hear the faint sound of children giggling. My mind scrabbles at her comment. Does she mean she wouldn't mind sleeping with someone who has children, in general? Or does she mean Tom?

'Don't look so shocked,' she says. 'He's good-looking. that's all. You've got to realise things have been hard on him.'

'What do you mean?'

'*You*,' she says. 'The poor man can't do a thing right. You're so idealistic. It has to be organic food, live music and no CDs, no plastic toys, no television, not even *Play School*. Everything he does is *wrong*. You wouldn't even let him wear dark clothing around the children, for God's sake.'

'Yes, I'm extreme. I know. I'm extreme,' I say, mostly to myself, digging my fingernails into my wrist. There's something else going on here, something she's not saying.

'A man likes things to be easygoing. Enjoyable. You shouldn't make things so hard.'

What's so wrong with being idealistic, I wonder irritably. How is it *hard*? Children should live in a gentle world. That's all.

'Do you think if I lightened up, he might come back?'

'That's not the feeling I got.'

So. She has inside knowledge. Why, that's what I want to know. She and Tom have never been close.

'You've talked to him about it, then?'

'Yes – he came over,' Paisley says, and smiles. 'We had a bottle of Beaujolais, actually.'

I jump out of the chair, knocking over my glass. It smashes on the floor. 'You're sleeping with him! You're sleeping with him, aren't you?'

I'm almost screaming but I can't help it; I'm bending over her, my hands are shaking her shoulders. She's shouting – *Get off!* – when I catch sight of a little face behind the glass door. Walter.

I leap back and slap my hands to my eyes, disgusted with myself. Taking a deep breath, I open the door.

'What is it?' I ask quietly.

He won't speak to me, of course. He runs to Paisley and starts crying. From further down the corridor, I can hear Opal and Joseph laughing hysterically. I march up the hallway and, seeing the bathroom light on, push open the door.

'What the hell's going on in here?' I bellow but stop short, open-mouthed. From the rim of the bath, the children look up at me with gleeful faces. Inside the bath, which they have managed to fill on their own, is a penguin. He swims around and around, flapping his tiny wings desperately, staring up at me with eyes like polished buttons.

Paisley and Walter have gone. She left the port-a-cot behind. I'm still angry and anxious, but a part of me is sorry that she's missed the penguin, that we don't share the *how on earth did they get it here?* conversation, nor the laughing until our sides ache at the children's cunning, nor the urgent discussion of what to do with him now and how to return him tomorrow. All this I do in my head. Except the laughing.

I lie awake in bed, pain raging in my arms and neck. I think about what Paisley said. And worse, what I did. The shaking of her. The *attack*. I didn't give the woman a chance. She's interested in Tom, and maybe flirting with him. They might even be together. This possibility makes me want to kick him where it hurts. But I force myself to consider it. And the more I explore it, the more I feel something else uncoiling; a deliciously self-righteous anger which – if I'm honest – is much easier to feel than rejection.

So there I am, in the weird loop of inner monologue at three in the morning: I replay the fight with Paisley, only in my fantasy version of events she confesses and apologises, full of shame, while I experience a sweet sense of vindication. This is sadly short-lived. Imagining them together makes me wretchedly low. Our sanctuary has been broken into, robbed and wrecked. But what if nothing's going on? Then all I've done is humiliate myself.

I soothe myself with the thought that Tom might still love me, and it all starts again with variations. I'm driving myself mad. I sit up in bed and throw off the covers. The house is so quiet; there's no noise outside or inside.

The penguin. I can't hear the penguin at all. What if he's fallen asleep and drowned in that inch of water I left in the bath? Tomorrow plagues my thoughts. I can't go at sunset and have people watch me *return* a penguin. No way. Better to go early, and surreptitiously release him at the water's edge… But will he know to swim off and join his friends? I picture him standing there at the wrong time of day. He might be confused. Until now, he's never been in the wrong place at the wrong time in his entire life. Nothing can prepare him for the shock of tomorrow.

At five o'clock I get up to check on him in the bathroom. I switch on the light and he shudders at the sudden brightness. Kneeling at the edge of the bath like a supplicant, I take a closer look. They used to call his kind fairy penguins. He looks at me out of his reflective eye. I touch him and find feathers almost like scales.

He doesn't move. He looks hypnotised; perhaps afraid. I can't tell. His penguin consciousness is as incomprehensible to me as my consciousness is to him. He's vivid and handsome and somehow dense, a compressed expression of being. How basic and rhythmic is his existence, how beautiful his design.

Slowly, I stand up and turn on the shower. Hot water might soothe my aching neck and arms. Wary of the penguin's hooked bill, I turn on the cold tap for the penguin too, before easing myself out of my pyjamas and into the tub. I crouch under the shower, my hair getting wet, leaning my forehead against the tiles. The tub begins to fill, and the penguin splashes and circles and yelps as the water deepens, a salty smell rising from his feathers.

Limp and damp, I haul myself back into bed and sleep soundly. At seven, Opal and Joseph wake me up, demanding to know why Walter isn't here. Joseph goes to the kitchen and the smoky stench of burnt bread forces me out of bed. Joseph's raisin toast stands in a crumbly black stack on the bench. He watches closely as I turn the knob down on the machine. Opal lifts the lid of the butter dish and dips in a finger.

'Let's set the table,' I say with false cheerfulness. This morning I'm bloated and sodden, a grey sea sponge that needs squeezing out.

At eight-thirty, as I'm making sandwiches to take on our return journey to Phillip Island, I hear shrieks of joy.

'Daddy's here, Daddy's here!'

My heart leaps in its old ritual of anticipating him. Just a hug, that's all. A hug would do a lot for me, right now.

They open the front door. 'Daddy, come and see! We've got a penguin in the bath.'

'Oh really?' I hear Tom say, playing along. 'A penguin?' The children laugh, delighted. They skip around him. 'Come and see, Daddy. Come and *see*.'

Some moments later, Tom appears in the kitchen. I can tell by his face there'll be no hugging. My knife doesn't miss a beat on the chopping block, blonde wafers of cheese appearing under the blade.

'Well,' he says. 'You're in a pretty pickle with that penguin.'
'I'll sort it out.'
'Paisley rang this morning.'

I raise my face towards him. His gaze is steady and serious. A boyish lock of hair has fallen over his forehead; he's rumpled and unshaven.

'So?' I say.

'You can't assault people like that, Rachel.'

I'm too angry to speak. I squeeze the knife handle and look down at the cheese. I can hear the children clattering in the bathroom.

'There's nothing going on. She understands what you're like. We chat. That's it.'

'Oh yeah? And what *am* I like?' I cry, dropping the knife on the bench. Tom shakes his head.

The children return to the kitchen and the conversation ends. Joseph, wearing his sheepskin mittens, holds the penguin. The bird is squawking, lunging its bill and leaving a trail of inky scat.

'Quick, get the knapsack!' he says.

'Careful kids,' says Tom, watching but not intervening. 'He might bite.'

Like an expert, Opal holds the knapsack open beneath the penguin, and they slide him hastily inside, giving me an unexpected glimpse into the shenanigans that must have gone on yesterday. Even in my agitated state this strikes me as funny. I make a strange humphing noise as I picture their coordinated kidnapping. Joseph stares at me, an uncertain half-smile on his lips.

'He did bite me, Dad,' says Joseph, holding up his mitted hand to show us the split in the sheepskin. 'It didn't get my skin.'

'It was wrong to take him,' says Tom. 'I hope your mother explained that.'

'Of course I did,' I say, slapping buttered bread over the cheese. 'Didn't I, kids?'

'Okay, take him out to the car,' says Tom. 'Listen Rach, we really have to talk.' But when he sees me grimace as I lift a heavy pan of water off the stove, he says: 'Why don't you buy wrist bands or supports for the arms? They might help.'

'I've made a doctor's appointment.'

'The doctor? I've told you: go and see Blodwyn.'

Blodwyn is a close friend of Tom and a chiropractor. I shrug. I've met her – she's nice enough. But I don't know if I want help from Tom's friends right now.

'What are you doing here, anyway? Shouldn't you be at work?' Rain clatters on the roof. The colours inside the kitchen soften and dim. I pour coffee into two cups and add milk to mine. 'What do you have to tell me?'

By the time I get the children into the car it's nearly ten o'clock. Joseph tucks the knapsack beside him and the car rolls over the gravel driveway, past the camellias and gums, and out onto the wet dirt road. To the right I see my landlords, Con and Julita, distant specks among the cows. We live in a cottage on their property, close to the road.

With my window open, I breathe in the wet earth fragrance lifting off the soil and flowers. We drive a mile or so over the dirt road and turn, crossing the bridge. Beneath it flows the Yarra River, fat and brown and glistening like an eel.

We head out towards the freeway, singing nursery rhymes. We'll go a different way today, and catch the ferry. Joseph tells Opal a story about the Billy Goats Gruff that he learned at kinder. Maybe the bridge reminded him. A green sign reads 'Seaford' and my hands tug the steering wheel. Will I go and see Dad? He's not the best person to talk to – sometimes he makes me feel even worse – but we haven't seen him for so long and he's all I've got right now. Why else would I have come this way?

Tom's news isn't quite what I expect. I'm hoping he'll tell me something more about why he'd left. He unwraps the plastic from the newspaper while he drinks his coffee.

'Remember the book proposal I sent that publisher? Well, they're interested. They want a draft in three months.'

I do a quick calculation. He needs to travel for research. He'll be away until Christmas. I try to animate my voice.

'That's great! It'll get you off the political round.'

'I like the political round,' he protests.

'Come on Tom, you're over it,' I say. 'How many times have you said that?'

'Yeah – I am,' he admits, sheepishly. 'But I don't think we can do this.'

He turns another page of the newspaper and puts a piece of fruit bread in the toaster. He isn't reading; his eyes dart over the page and his left leg twitches the way it does when he's thinking about something. He's tall and dark, with a thick scar running from his jaw to the outside tip of his eyebrow. He always eats breakfast standing up, reading the paper or a travel book, putting toast in, boiling the kettle, writing lists on scraps of paper.

'There's our … situation. And your arms aren't good. It can't be easy looking after the children.'

'It isn't. But now you've left me it'll make little difference if you're in the country or not.'

Tom sighs, rubbing at the space between his eyebrows. 'It's all a mess. The thing is, Rachel, if I take two months without pay, I'll need a loan from my folks to pay rent, and for you guys to have food. You haven't made much lately.'

I shrug. 'So? Just do it. Get the loan.'

'But you've always been against us borrowing money from them!'

'I didn't want us to depend on them. But it doesn't matter now. And anyway, this is a once-in-a-lifetime chance.'

'I haven't told them about us splitting.'

'What?' I say, surprised. 'But you're staying there, in the campervan?'

'I told them it was so I could write. If I'm going to ask them for money, I don't want to tell them.'

'You want to lie.'

'Not exactly. Maybe just, you know, pick our time.'

Driving through the sunny bayside streets of Seaford, we pass the old milk bar with mirrored windows where my friends and I once bought paper bags of one-cent lollies; milk bottles and teeth, and bright yellow bananas which smelt like paint thinner if you left them in the sun.

At Dad's street, I feel nervous. I've only seen him a few times since Mum died and he always says the same thing. *Life never touches you, sweetheart. You've never needed anyone's help,* as though what happened in our family didn't happen to me, only to him.

'Where are we?' says Joseph. 'This isn't Phillip Island.'

'We're at Grandpa's.'

Dad's ute is in the driveway. I climb out of the car and unbuckle the children, lifting Opal onto my hip. Joseph puts on his knapsack.

'How's the penguin?'

'He's asleep.'

This is not where I grew up. When my mother died my father moved to this cheap hole. In the frame of one large window a mattress is wedged. In the other the glass is intact but latticed with cracks. Between them, the open front door is dark like a missing tooth. The front yard is a mass of weeds. An old rose climbs over the front verandah, a single, beer-coloured bloom hanging onto a stem as tough as cowhide.

Inside, the house smells of fried bacon. I can hear a radio. Joseph puts his hand in mine. On one side is the bedroom, where there's a dusty sleeping bag and a pile of fishing magazines, and a white enamel basin with a razor beside it, filled with ginger stubble.

The bathroom on the right has no sink, just a curtainless shower and a toilet with no seat or lid. Mould flowers thickly over the walls. The next room is a living room, which has an old couch and a coffee table with a sculpture on it. My first real piece, one of a woman kneeling, handless arms stretching forwards, the work that got me into art school. I thought it had been lost years ago. Why would he have that here, I wonder.

'I don't like that lady, Mummy,' says Opal, into my ear.

'She's not real. Mummy made her out of clay, a long, long time ago.'

By the dirty light coming through the smeared window, I catalogue the mistakes: the head bending forward incorrectly, the flat shoulders, and of course, the missing hands. How I'd agonised over those knuckles and fingers! Dad had teased me about them so much that in the end I sliced them off with a piece of wire, taking pleasure as I did so. No more hours of sculpting – the relief was exquisite. The examiners would have to take it or leave it.

'Come on,' I say to Joseph, tugging his hand gently. Opal buries her head into my shoulder.

'Hungry,' she whispers, rubbing her tummy.

The kitchen bench is covered with empty cans: beer, mushrooms and beans, even sausages. Through the back window I can see his shaved head, the sort of pinky-brown skin of a labourer, overlaid with a greenish cast made by the plastic roof of the porch. He's listening to footy talkback.

The fly-wire door squeaks but he doesn't turn. There's a huge concrete mixer with a fire burning in it. He's placed a grill over the top and laid strips of bacon across it. With one hand he turns the bacon with tongs, with the other he's playing Solitaire on a little card table. There's a beer already open.

'Hi Dad,' I say.

He glances over his shoulder. 'Jesus Christ,' he says impassively; nothing ever surprises him. 'It's the skinny bitch.'

'Nice to see you too, Dad.'

We walk into his domain. Out on the grass, a television flickers on a bookshelf balanced against an old bed frame, next to the radio. Electric cords are piled onto double adaptors leading back to the house.

Joseph's eyes are popping at the sight of Dad's stuff: the saucepans hanging from nails on the trellis, buckets full of fishing tackle, rolled sheafs of sandpaper, a hammer and six screwdrivers hanging next to the saucepans, a workbench for planing wood, a saw, a silver-lipped axe, a plastic tub full of inner tubes and the skeletal remains of bike frames he's dragged home from someone's hard rubbish collection, a big brown bottle labelled 'TURPS' in black texta, old biscuit and cigarette tins now rusting. One or two of these tins have the lids off and inside there are batteries, nuts and bolts, and pulleys. Dad picks one up and offers it to Joseph.

'Wanna take a look, son? What's ya name again?'

'Joseph.'

'Joseph! That's my name! Most people call me Joe.'

'How could you forget that, Dad?' I snap. 'Your own name.'

'Just stirrin',' he says. 'Y'always bite.'

Walking over to the precarious bookshelf, passing an upturned bathtub covered with books and ornaments, I turn off the radio and the television. Kerri-Anne Kennerley's face disappears.

'Still raising the kids like pansies?' says Dad. 'Can't get rid of Kerri-Anne. She's the closest thing I've got to a wife.'

'Nice to switch her off then.'

He grins and throws a couple of pieces of white bread onto the grill. Though well into his sixties, his cut-off checked shirt reveals sinewy muscle covered with fur and freckles, a shape bequeathed to him by a lifetime working as a brickie. Opal wriggles down from my hip.

'Can I have something to eat?' she says to Dad.

'Please,' I say.

'Sure, sweetheart. You're pretty. You look just like your mother.'

Opal smiles, tucking a red-gold curl behind one ear. She is adorable in her little pink dress. My father spreads a yellow chunk of butter onto the warm bread and presses a sputtering piece of bacon inside.

'She'll just have the bread,' I say.

'She'll have what she's given,' he replies, glancing up at me with his eyes ever so slightly narrowed. Then he puckers his lips and says: 'Oooh Rachel, if you could see your face! Dying to give me what for. Still got ya temper.'

'You've still got your disrespect,' I reply. 'Anyway, they don't eat meat.'

'*They don't eat meat,*' he mimics. He hands one to Joseph. Hungry, the children devour their sandwiches, butter smearing their chins, eyes wide.

'Want to take home that tin, son? You could put it in your bag.'

'My bag's full,' says Joseph. 'It's got a penguin in it. We've got to take him home.'

'A penguin?'

Joseph stuffs the last of the bread and bacon into his mouth and kneels by his knapsack to unzip it. The penguin, thus unveiled, stands blinking in the sunlight. My father shakes his head, flabbergasted.

'Where the *hell* did ya get a fucking penguin?'

'Language, *Dad*!' I say, wincing. 'The first I knew of it was when I found him in the bath when we got home from Phillip Island.'

My father absorbs this information in silence. The children watch him, curious to see what he'll say. We all wait. He surprises us with a huge guffaw of laughter. His laugh goes up and down the scale like a hammer on chimes; his whole body shakes and ripples and he gives himself up to it, before wiping his eyes with the backs of his hands. The sound of his laughter, so warm and real and unexpected, fills me with happy memories.

'I'll be damned!'

He gets up and pushes the books and ornaments off the bathtub and turns it over.

'Get that hose, Joseph. Do you know how to turn it on? Opal, pass me that salt.'

In no time, my father's fed the penguin a tin of anchovies and got him swimming in a salty bath, the plughole stopped with Blu-Tack and a stone. I'd forgotten this about him, his gentle knack with animals, his ability to easily enlist others in a little project. I sit on a stool, watching him play with the children and the penguin, and I eat a piece of grilled bread with butter. The penguin seems less distressed.

'Do you want any of ya mum's stuff?' says Dad, gesturing

to the objects now scattered on the ground. 'They're pulling this place down this month they reckon, and I only want to take a suitcase out of here.'

So he kept a few things, I think, suddenly remembering the garbage bags my mother filled with clutter the day she died. There's a sketchpad with a few drawings, an old floral sunhat that I don't remember her wearing, vases she once filled with garden flowers. The wooden soldier nutcracker we used at Christmas is here, his mouth unhinged. A book of fairy tales she bought for me.

'I'll take this,' I say, drawing the book onto my lap and flicking open the front cover to read the inscription. But I change my mind — I don't want to read this now. I close the book, smoothing the wrinkles in the tatty cover, and pack it inside Opal's bag.

'How's Tom?' says Dad.

'He's left me,' I say, quietly enough that the children won't hear.

'Christ! That's a turn-up. Wouldn't have picked it,' he says, rubbing his chin. 'Still, you wouldn't be easy to live with. You inherited the worst from both of us. A perfectionist, like ya mother. With my temper.'

'He didn't say that's why he was leaving.'

'No,' says Dad. 'Well, he wouldn't, would he? Poor bugger wouldn't dare.'

'Thanks Dad, you're a real comfort.'

He shrugs and grins.

'We've got to get going, kids,' I say more loudly, glancing at my watch. 'We've got to get this little penguin home.'

'Leave the penguin with me,' my father says, standing up. 'I got a job down in Cowes from tomorrow. No trouble.'

'Oh – okay,' I say, feeling suddenly unburdened. 'Thanks Dad. That would really help me out.'

He walks us out to the front door. As the sculpture passes by the corner of my eye, I feel the shock of her presence. It's as though someone is there, gazing out from the living room. Before this moment I hadn't noticed how the long face with its hint of a smile, the graciously bowed head – incorrect technique notwithstanding – held so much of my mother. A benevolent word on her clay lips. Or a curse. Maybe that's why he's kept it. Not because he's proud of me but because it reminds him of her.

Driving out of Seaford, the rain starts up again. Water spatters over our car in the wake of a truck on the freeway. Rain pouring over the asphalt, the endless white lines, I can't wait to get off the freeway and be home, cuddled up with the children, telling stories.

'The rain's like crystals,' shouts Joseph, over the din.

My gaze settles briefly on the droplets coating the windscreen. I blink and watch traffic. I put the statue out of my mind and worry about the question of Tom. I want him back. Rarely inclined to give my father credit for insight, I wonder if he's on to something with the perfectionism jibe.

'You keep ridiculous standards,' Tom once told me, after I'd shouted at him for leaving his jacket on the floor.

'I'm trying to teach the children good habits. How will they ever learn to pick up their clothes if you leave yours everywhere?'

'It's just tedious, Rachel. Life's not like that.'

'*My* clothes are picked up. The house shines. The children eat at the same time every day. They *thrive* on routine. Then you come along and mess it all up.'

I remember Tom putting his head in his hands. 'You set yourself up for disappointment,' he said quietly. 'You're like a truck. You stop for nothing.'

Yes, I tell myself. I've worn him out. I could go and see him tonight, wear a pretty dress, get him to talk to me about how he feels. I could listen quietly, really *listen*. The babysitter could come – she doesn't charge much.

'I know a song about crystals,' calls Joseph from the back.

'Why don't you teach Opal? Her name is a kind of crystal.'

'Sing after me, Opes. Little crystal, where do you wander?'

'Little cwystal, where do you wander.'

'From one ca – ave to another.'

'On the ca – ave…'

'No, *from one* cave.'

In the industrial wasteland that flanks the freeway we pass a huge black bird that pecks at a piece of orange fibreglass. What is that meant to be? A piece of cheese, a hot chip? A witty comment on other public works? Because I'm a sculptor people ask my opinion. Whimsy, I shrug. Like pieces from a child's board game. Decorations of an impish culture obsessed with exteriority. We like the thing itself, not what lies behind it.

The rain continues its bright and noisy clatter over the roof of the car as we head into Warrandyte.

'Mummy, I'm hungry,' says Opal, a whine creeping into her voice. I glance into the rear-view mirror and see her tired face. No wonder, with all the excitement over the penguin last night. She needs a nap.

'Nearly home now, sweetie,' I say soothingly. It was the usual time for her afternoon tea.

'I'm hungry!'

'But you had a sandwich at Grandpa's.'

Under the bridge, the Yarra burbles and twists, stung and dimpled with rain. I take it slow down our unmade road, knowing the troughs will have filled up. We slosh down one of them and get stuck. *Shit*.

I have no choice but to step into ankle-deep water. The mud swills into my shoes as I walk to the back of the car and push. Pain sears my wrists. The car won't budge. I get back inside and try reversing, but all I hear is the sound of the back tyres spinning and splattering the boot with mud.

'What's happening?' asks Joseph. 'Are we *bogged*?'

'Mummy, I'm really, really hungry,' says Opal.

Wordlessly, I get out of the car and try again to push, and this time the children climb out, too. I didn't even know Opal could undo her seatbelt.

'Get back into the car this instant! You're just going to get muddy.'

'No!' pouts Opal.

I open the door and point. 'Get back in right now or you're in big trouble.'

Suddenly, my phone rings. It's Ruth. *Don't answer*. But if

I don't, she'll know I'm avoiding her. Just do it quickly, get it over and done.

'Rachel! Why haven't you been answering my calls?'

'Oh Ruth, I'm so sorry,' I say, gesticulating furiously at Opal to get back in the car. 'I've had a bit of a hold-up.'

'I've got buyers waiting!'

'I know. I'm seeing a doctor tomorrow.'

Opal sits down in the mud and starts crying. 'I'm *hungry*!'

I cover the mouthpiece. 'Yes,' I hiss. 'You *know* I'd give you some food if I could!'

'What's going on?' says Ruth.

'Oh God, sorry Ruth – it's Opal, she...'

'But you'll be ready for the exhibition next week?'

'The work won't be done, I'm sorry...'

'*What?*' The frustration she packs into that one word is exceptional.

'I'm sorry,' I mumble.

'I've got half a dozen artists who'd kill for your spot. I stuck my neck out for you!'

The rain is falling fast now. Opal is getting drenched in her flimsy dress.

'Opal, get back into the car!'

'No.'

'You're a naughty girl!' I shriek. 'Why don't you *do* what Mummy says? Ruth...? Are you there?'

'Mummy,' says Joseph, tugging my arm gently. 'I need to go to the toilet. So I'm just going over there, okay?'

He's *managing* me. Ruth's hung up. My career's in a coma and I'm in a strange zone somewhere between dazed and furious. Joseph runs off into the muddy field to a tree that he imagines hides him, and squats. Opal is, by now, screaming. She's red faced, throwing handfuls of mud around. I keep out of range.

'Please be quiet,' I say, knowing it's futile.

'I couldn't wipe my bottom,' Joseph says, coming up beside me, embarrassed.

'That's okay, sweetheart, we'll fix it at home,' I say, trying to regain my composure. *She hung up on me, that bloody snobbish spray-tanned bitch-head. After all the work I've done for her. Years of my life.*

'Hop back in the car. I have to call the mechanic.'

As I say this, I see a pile of old fence palings from where Con's pulled a fence down.

'Actually, Joe – come give Mummy a hand,' I say.

We drag the palings over and wedge them under the front and back wheels. Opal stops screaming and watches. As a reward for his help, I tell Joseph he can sit in the front seat. I put Opal beside him, not wanting to start fresh trouble.

'I'm sorry for shouting, darling — Mummy lost her temper. We'll be eating muffins at home very, very soon,' I say, shaking the water off my hair and brow. I turn the key in the ignition and after a few readjustments we're out of there. With my knees caked with mud and my shoes full of squelch, I drive onto the shoulder where the road's firmer, and slowly but surely we make our way home.

I don't act on my plan to see Tom; I can't risk the car getting bogged again and I feel shaken after the incident with Opal. Instead I creep into bed, a chastened woman, and read fairy tales. The sweet, stubby shape of the penguin materialises in my thoughts. Only now do I realise that a part of me was looking forward to returning him to his true place, to saying farewell.

In the end, I have to put down the book: it hurts too much to hold it. My wrists are cold and throbbing. I lie the phone handset on the pillow next to my ear and press Ruth's number on quick dial, before resting my hands on cushions. She's not there and I can't think of a message to leave.

I switch off my lamp. Through the open curtains the moon is absent, snuffed by the world's shadow, yet the stars sparkle and glimmer and flicker on and on, holy sky flames.

Are we really made of the same stuff as the stars? I heard that somewhere. It seems unlikely.

Only a week ago, I'd be waiting for Tom, listening to him huff and sigh as he tapped at the keyboard of his laptop, followed by the computer shutting down in four mechanised beats. Footsteps along the carpeted hallway. Rattling the lock on the front door. More footsteps. A toilet flush, the shower turned on for a few minutes, then off, the sound of teeth-brushing. He'd finally arrive in bed, wrapped in a fresh towel over clean, warm skin, his weight depressing the mattress beside me. I'd be almost asleep – almost, but not quite. Faint needles of starlight would prickle over us as we nestled into each other. His chin pressing into my shoulder, sometimes his lips. The very first time Tom kissed me the word I thought of was *pressure*; an irresistible pressure. I am his clay, his bread, as he is mine. Now that I don't have his physical pressure there is another kind: absence. Absence is not the opposite of presence. Absence is a pressure coming from the self.

Blodwyn's place looks more like an English cottage than a chiropractic clinic. She is Welsh, after all; a tall Welsh woman with white-blonde hair whose accent sounds almost Indian. Her clinic is close by, in the main strip of town.

The sunny morning dried the worst puddles on our road and we got here without incident; the three of us are now walking through an enchanted garden of daffodils, tulips, lavender and roses. Beside the door, engraved on what looks like a recycled fence paling is a sign which reads 'Blodwyn Tarrant. Chiropractor'. And above the door, on a similar piece of wood, are the words 'All who dwell here are safe'.

A plump woman with crinkled brown eyes greets me at reception. 'You can leave your children with me,' she says, smiling.

'Oh no – can't they come in?'

Already Opal and Joseph have made their way to the corner. A muslin cloth has been half pulled back to reveal wooden chairs around a little table and tiny kitchen implements and a doll in a highchair.

'It's better for you if they don't.'

Stepping through the doorway, I see Blodwyn standing by the window, partly in silhouette. The room is warm, with three chiropractic couches in chocolate leather and a real fire in the grate. Her teak desk has very little on it; several sheets of paper, a pen, and a vase of garden flowers. There's not much else in the room except a basket of flannel face-cloths, a chair and a single beeswax candle burning on the mantelpiece. There's no picture on the wall, no inspirational quotes, no incense, no computer or CD player, no family photograph.

Blodwyn hugs me. 'How are you?' she asks. Thickset and plain-looking by modern standards, a closer look reveals a broad face with fair skin and delicate concertinas of laugh lines around her mouth.

'Sort of okay,' I say, shuffling sideways. 'Do I sit on one of these couches?'

'Sure. Tom told me about your arms.'

She's standing behind me. With knowing precision, she presses a fingertip into a sore spot in my shoulder. I gasp. Blodwyn spreads a face-cloth over the couch and pats it. I lie down, my face wedged between the planks of leather under the cloth.

'Breathe,' she says softly and presses my back here and there. 'Ah. Yes. Try making a little noise now, Rachel.'

When I open my lips, a strangled groan comes out.

'It doesn't sound very nice,' I protest.

'No one can hear you.'

'The children.'

Blodwyn crosses the room, linen tunic swishing, and closes the door. 'Connect to the pain,' she says. 'Make the sound. Give it a colour and a texture. Does it bring up any memories? What are they? What were your needs, then?'

'I just need my hands to work *now*. I have so much to do. Everything in my life is my hands.'

'What if I told you your hands will never get better?'

I'm stunned by the tears that suddenly spring into my eyes, unbidden. I've never considered this possibility. To be in pain every time I ever did anything: cook, clean, sew, sculpt, carry children... My will would be thwarted at every turn.

'Are you less loveable without the use of your hands?' she asks, softly.

'Of course!' The words fly out of my mouth. I stop myself from saying the rest: I am nothing if I cannot *do*. I do things, that's how I am. I don't need help. I help others. I don't need help.

'Make the sound, Rachel.'

Underneath the couch is a pillow. I grab it and push my face down into it to muffle the keening howls, a kind of strangulated scream that I make several times, interspersed with ugly gasps.

My mind's eye penetrates the interior of my arms to see the colour of the pain: dark red. The texture is claggy. Brown, slug-like tendrils of pain unfurl from my elbows to my wrists and hands, slowly, ineffably, grotesquely knitting themselves around the veins, the fine bones.

A memory surfaces. I'm in the back room at Seaford, kneeling on the cold floor, scrubbing blood from the floorboards. Most of the blood is dry and doesn't loosen easily. I scrub and scrub. My hands and arms are aching and I'm sweating all over, but I swear I'll get that blood off so Dad doesn't have to see it again. And I do.

'I've had enough now,' I announce to Blodwyn, sitting up a little too quickly.

'Take it easy. You'll get a head-rush,' she says, carrying a bowl of warm water that's materialised from somewhere. She hands me a flannel and I wash my face, grateful. She's on my side. She's *for* me in a way no one else is. And she barely knows me.

'Did you remember something?'

'Yes, but I don't want to talk about it,' I say. 'Did Tom tell you we've split up?'

'Yes.'

'Well, I've worked out why. I've driven him away with my perfectionism. So I'm going to tell him I'll change.'

'That sounds like a plan,' says Blodwyn. I look at her quickly.

'*That* sounds like a deliberately neutral comment.'

Blodwyn laughs. 'Are you ready to give it up?'

'Give up what?'

'Your perfectionism, as you call it. That's what got you this far in life, isn't it?'

'Sure, I'm ready,' I shrug. 'No big deal.'

Here I stand like a thief in a silver dress, before one of the most elaborate mansions on Montalto Avenue. The curved driveway is paved with loose stones, white and flat. I pick one up and turn it over and over, nervously. I'm going to tell him everything. Beg him to come home. What if he says no? *Don't think about that. Listen to what he has to say. Don't hog all the talking space.*

Shimmering light spills out of the huge bay window in the dining room. The stones make an abominable crunching underfoot and I skip onto the smooth lawn, pressing myself into the flowerbed under the window to peek inside. The curly twigs of a crazy philbert tree scratch my cheeks. Mr and Mrs Welford are dining on the oval table, under the chandelier. Tom isn't with them. He will be in the campervan around the back. Or out.

Curly twigs have caught my hair. I spend several tense minutes untwining the strands. Once disentangled, I keep to the shadows and let myself through the side gate, hoping – praying, if I'm honest – the dogs are indoors eating their dinner.

The campervan's small square windows are yellow with electric light and I rehearse under my breath. *Sorry, Tom, for being so uncompromising and hot-tempered. Sorry for my big mouth. Sorry I wore you out with ideals that have become too rigid. Please come back. We miss you.*

It's not until I get to the little door – my hand literally raised to knock – that I hear a woman's voice. Taking a step back I stand on tiptoes and peep through the window. Tom and Paisley are sitting on armchairs. Between them is a foldable table with a fringed lamp, a bottle of red and two glasses of wine. My hand clenches around the stone and breath whistles over my clamped teeth. If you could reduce yourself to your essence at any moment, what would you be? A mute cry, a mash of dirty green light? *You're an idiot, Rachel.*

Paisley's wearing black with white silk knotted loosely at the throat and a mouth as red as a poppy. Tom looks dishevelled in his unironed favourite *Big Lebowski* T-shirt. He hasn't brushed his hair. It's obvious from the animated discussion that they're talking about something interesting. Paisley leans forward and touches Tom's scar. She's asking him about it. I can hear the bell-like timbre of her voice, though not the words themselves. I've never told her what my mother did. Tom rubs the scar and she withdraws her hand, though she's still leaning forward, the skin over her collarbones glowing like polished white clay. He's telling her the story and she looks shocked. It *is* shocking.

They sit back, silent. Paisley swigs her wine, Tom rolls and lights a spliff, draws back and hands it to her. With narrowed eyes I watch as she sucks it back in the sexiest way I've ever seen. Paisley, who never smokes, and Tom, who's supposedly given up years ago. The sour, leafy smell leaks under the door.

I turn the stone over in my hand. *Bitch*. Paisley leans forward again, lips parted because she's going to kiss him, I can see it coming. She's moving closer and he doesn't move away, he's watching her dumbly as she leans into him, a hand on his knee, pressing her mouth against his. Hot wrath seizes me and I throw the stone, hard, into the window.

The glass shatters. Paisley shrieks and Tom yells out, 'Hey!' I must have hit her. *Shit*.

I take off – not back up the driveway and out towards my car like a person who thinks under pressure, but deep into the garden, my heels sinking into the earth. I'm wearing the wrong shoes.

Kicking them off, I plunge into the agapanthus bushes, which push against me with their springy vegetable force. Damned weeds, why don't my in-laws get their gardener to plant light, feathery plants, they've got the money – they stink of it. Lights come on at the back of the house. The back door swings open. A dog barks.

The dogs will find me. I force the shoes into my handbag and scramble up the back fence, ignoring the pain in my arms. I slide down the other side into someone else's backyard. Sensor lights suddenly illuminate a swimming pool.

I race to the side fence. It's made of double brick, broad enough for me to run along, past the blazing lights to the front yard, where, half jumping and half sliding, I make it safely to the ground, startling a possum on her way up. What if they call the police? Oh please, no. I sprint along the quiet street, searching for the car keys with my fingers, shoes tumbling out of the bag. No, don't leave a shoe, don't leave any trace. My hair! On the crazy philbert. Forensic scientists will find that, for sure.

No one's got to my car before me and I drive off like the mad woman I am, my heart shuddering. My slippery fingers slide over the wheel; I run a red light, doing ninety in a sixty zone.

At home, I pay Mandy and watch her cross the fields back to her place with a torch. I soak a flannel and scrub my face with long strokes until every flake of the hoped-for seduction is removed. Standing before the mirror, I peel away the dress like a silver wrapping and drop it to the floor. Reddened and shamed, I look into my own eyes. Unclad, raw, a cow-herding girl – but not even a girl any more: the matron is coming for me with her arms of cosy fat. My skin is drying like the pages of a manuscript lettered with childbirth, lovemaking, nicotine and alcohol, and under it all the bones are losing density. But the letters of my true being are not written here; I am not only my body. I've never believed that yet here I am mourning it, sucked into that great big lie, measuring myself by flesh more than ever.

Tom was lying about not liking Paisley. We were renting a clapped-out weatherboard in the inner city when we got to know her. We were married by then. I'd dropped out of university and worked as a waitress by day, sculpting at night, and Tom was doing his Masters in English Literature. Paisley was studying music. We grew snow peas and tomatoes and kept chickens; they squawked softly as we lay on the grass and drank beer.

'So why *do* you call me your little cow-herding girl?' I asked Tom.

'Because you're a bogan who didn't finish her education!' He laughed as I pummelled him with my fists, but he kept going: 'An unlettered desert-tribe girl with bad manners.'

'Thanks very much!' I shouted.

And Paisley said, 'But remember Tom, she may be *low caste, ill mannered and dirty, but the god took the fruit she'd been sucking.*'

Tom sat up and brushed dirt and chicken dung from his jeans, staring at Paisley. How I envied her knowing tone, her graceful neck, the blue shimmer in her hair.

'Since when have you been able to quote sixteenth-century bhakta poets?' he asked, smiling.

Paisley raised an immaculate eyebrow at me, as if to say, *showed him a thing or two.* She was covering herself, but I didn't miss the little frisson that passed between them.

The light is flat and lucid by the Yarra this morning, and the mud is welcome, even encouraged; Joseph and Opal are wearing their oldest clothes and making mud pies with the intensity of the inspired. They press pebbles and leaves into the black shapes; when the earth dries too much they sprinkle it with Yarra water. I lie beside them on a picnic blanket with a basket full of fruit and sandwiches and cookies and drinks, nursing my throbbing arms and broken heart – and hiding from Tom.

If I let them make shapes from the earth for hours and days, will they learn reverence for nature and themselves?

The question floats through my mind dully. It's the kind of thought that has consumed me since Joseph's birth, when I found myself in the scission between holy newborn and brutal world. At this moment, however, the thought hovers with no force or colour, present as a memory of what preoccupied me before Tom left, when everything was hallowed by my love for them.

I feel him before I see him. Sitting up, I observe the familiar walk – a nonchalant, long-legged saunter – the hair falling over his forehead, hands deep in the pockets of his coat, kicking the gravel beside plum trees whitely veiled with blossom. He looks up and when he sees I'm watching him, he ducks and holds up his hands.

'Don't throw stones at me,' he says, with an uneven smile.

Straightening, I tuck my hair behind my ears and, in the obtuse hope of finding a shred of dignity, I say: 'I don't know what you're talking about.'

'Don't give me that, Rachel. I *saw* you running past the driveway. Like a nutter. Wearing some kind of silver ball-gown. What were you *doing*?'

'Is Paisley all right?' I ask.

'Nothing they couldn't stitch up in casualty.'

'Stitches. Casualty. God.'

My head drops to my knees, pulled up before me.

'You're lucky you didn't cause more damage,' he says, as a muddy Opal slides onto his lap, nuzzling under his chin.

'You should see my castle, Daddy,' calls Joseph. 'It's really a fort!'

'When you weren't at home I thought I might find you here,' Tom says. 'Of course, it would be easier if Mummy left her phone on.'

I lie back on the picnic blanket and look at the sky. The wind picks up and I pull the edges of the blanket around me. Opal and Joseph drag Tom over to see their mud constructions; after a time he returns and opens the basket and helps himself. What are the boundaries to a picnic basket when you're no longer together? A reprimand comes to my lips, but I bite down on it. It isn't easy. Dad likes to say redheads are loudmouths but maybe, one day, life will beat it out of me.

'Did you tell her it was me?'

'Had to,' says Tom, crunching into an apple. 'Otherwise we would've had to call the cops and that wouldn't have been good for anyone.'

'So you're together.'

'Come on, you were there, you saw – I didn't invite her. She just arrived. Then you turned up! What did *you* come about?'

'Don't change the subject.'

'Paisley and I are not together, Rachel. Okay? But you and I aren't together, either.'

'Why? Why *aren't* we? You say you need space. Is it because I'm too much hard work?'

'Paisley did mention that, actually—'

'*Did she!*' I say, my voice full of sarcastic rage. 'I'm just wondering how it got to this, how you and *Paisley* are discussing our marriage. Why aren't *we* discussing it?'

'Calm down,' says Tom, his face drained. 'I'm trying to work things out without your constant interrogation.'

'Just – tell me. Just help me understand.'

'I don't know. I suppose … you've changed.'

'What do you mean?'

'It's like you're living by a set of rules or something.'

I chew my lip, looking at him. 'But how do I do that?'

Tom issues a noisy sigh. 'I don't know. You're obsessed with keeping things clean. I mean, you sweep the floor ten times a day, like it's saving your life.'

A memory surfaces of my mother cleaning. I'd crept unobserved into the kitchen to find her crouched in front of the cupboard under the sink, hurling out Jif empties and used Steelo soap pads as though ridding herself of something obscene.

'You've left me because I keep the house clean?'

Tom tosses the apple core into the scrub under the plum trees. The scents of dogs' urine and river mud are in the wind that shifts the blossom, causing it to drift lightly over his hair. By the water's edge, the children's backs are freckled with white petals.

'I want to spend a bit of time with the kids before I go away,' he says. 'On my own.'

'In the campervan?'

'No, I thought I'd come home,' he says. 'Less disruption for them.'

'And you want me to go, is that it?'

'Well … yes.'

'For how long?'

'A few days,' he says. Then, looking into my face with some kindness, he says, 'Just a night or two.'

'Fine. I'll go home and pack,' I say. 'But make sure they go to bed by seven. No sugar, no television…'

'I can take care of them,' says Tom, and I know his tone. If I don't shut up now there'll be a fight.

It's a reasonable request, but the idea of being separated from Joseph and Opal for two nights seems unbearable. I can't let this happen, I can't let this family that I held so dear, far above my work, be pulled away from me like a toy on a string. Tom gathers up the children, folding their muddy bodies under his coat, and I can hear their muffled giggling as they walk away.

'Take the picnic basket,' I call after them. They don't hear me.

Tom and I first met on the back seat of a Ford station wagon at around four in the morning. It was dark. A mutual friend, Julian, was driving a carload to a wedding in a seaside place called Shellhorn, north of Sydney. The couple was getting married under a jacaranda tree so extraordinarily large and beautiful they felt justified in asking Melbourne friends, mostly students too impoverished to fly, to make the fourteen-hour trip. Two years later, Tom and I married under the same tree.

Tom was the last to be picked up. In the automated flash of light before the car door closed, I glimpsed a face both youthful and craggy, long hair, long limbs. He sat beside me, smelling of peppermint toothpaste and nightclub denim, and in the dark we talked about politics and films. He seemed impressed that I was studying sculpture.

'I've never met a sculptress before.'

'A sculptor,' I corrected. 'And I'm not one yet, just trying to be. Actually, I'm thinking of dropping out.'

'Sculptress is a nice word, though. I guess it's sexist, is it?'

Outside the car, night softened its grip. We were beyond the city, traversing the bland highway; on either side of us were deep, grey fields filled with ghostly huddles of sheep. The other passengers were dozing.

'Let me see, I memorised a poem at school about a sculptor,' Tom said, musing. '*The obstinate block, mere weight, oppressed his hands that sought and failed to find what lay within...*'

'That's Judith Wright,' I said, smiling.

'You *absolute* show-off,' said Julian from the front seat, punctuating each word with disapproval. 'You know he's got a photographic memory, Rachel, and he uses it to pick up girls?'

'Who cares if he's showing off if he's showing something beautiful?' I'm cross with Julian for interrupting the moment.

Behind Tom, first light was rising. I still couldn't see his face, only the rough-hewn edge of his cheek. But as the road curved, sunlight moved from left to right, peeling shadow from a face like that of an unfinished god. I stared. My hands itched to press themselves over the bumpy contours of lip and brow and dip into the philtrum as broad as a thumbprint; to smooth the planes of this face that was to become so beloved.

Ruth Stannard's inner-city gallery sits at the corner of two main roads, a taupe-coloured Victorian terrace with latticework. A spiky row of natives in terracotta pots rests on the tessellated tiles. A painting of a cow by Miller dominates the front window.

The sky is uncertain, a pavilion of ashy clouds streaked with blue. An hour behind me are Joseph and Opal in the sole care of their father; I'm barely myself without them, wobbling up the tiled pathway, holding my one finished lump of clay.

Opening the front door, I pass the gallery on the right and walk up the hallway, the wistful eyes of Butler's maidens watching from the walls. The desk is unoccupied in Ruth's sleek waiting room; Marco's probably out getting soy lattes in a cardboard tray. There are hushed voices from Ruth's office. Music is playing and I recognise Lisa Gerrard's *The Silver Tree*. One of my sculptures balances elegantly on the granite table as though it drifted there. Ruth purchased it in the early days of our relationship, when she was my tireless champion. I'd modelled it on a piece of coral with literally hundreds of rounded extrusions, each polished to the palest oyster grey with the back of a teaspoon. It was made before the children came and now I wonder whether such an object will ever be made by these hands again.

Thankfully, the sofa is soft and I sink into it, releasing the clay which rests on my lap. Stretching my hands out of their claw-like gesture, there is burning string between my thumb and my elbow. I pull out my tiger balm, and though its scent is anti-social, I rub it into my wrist anyway.

Ruth's door opens and she emerges, a slick fifty-year-old in a red shirt-dress, jet beads and glossy, espresso-brown tresses. Marco follows her out, sharp and neat in charcoal silk. They appraise me before speaking, as is the habit of these people.

'Finally, you're here,' says Ruth.

'Yes,' I say, standing up.

Ruth watches me. She seems to turn up her nose slightly – perhaps at the smell of the tiger balm. 'You're overwhelmed at the moment, aren't you, Rachel.' Her voice is crisp. Her business-like manner is what I've valued in her as an agent; but now I'm not so good for business: my stocks are down and she knows it. 'Perhaps it's time we part ways for a bit,' she says. 'You know how busy it is. Maybe get in touch when you're working again.'

Inside her office, I glimpse my clay fans and seashells spread out next to a spool of bubble wrap. Wearily, I pick up my offering from where I left it on the sofa. The burning in my right arm intensifies, shoots down the ring finger and under the fingernail.

'Fine,' I say.

I just don't feel like fighting for it. Tears run down my cheeks and, holding my parcel, I can't wipe them away.

The three of us stand there, an awkward clover of silence interrupted only by my sniffling. Marco takes my parcel and hands me a handkerchief, very soft, made of something like cotton lawn and emblazoned with an embroidered M.

'Keep it,' he says, as I hesitate, not wanting to soil it.

'Can we look at this?' says Ruth, tapping the parcel, curiosity getting the better of her.

'Sure,' I say.

Marco unwraps my one finished piece, a double clamshell I copied from one at the beach. It's not in the same league as the coral but it is very exact, each fine, shining groove widening and then graduating inwards again at the edge. Marco lays it on the granite coffee table.

'Opal said it looked like angel's wings,' I say, swiping my cheeks rather aggressively with the hanky.

'This is what I'm talking about,' says Marco, raising his plucked eyebrows. 'No one's doing work like this.'

'I can't carry her if she's *not* working,' says Ruth.

'She just has to get her arms stronger,' says Marco. He turns to me. 'You can get them fixed, can't you?'

What if I told you your hands will never get better?

'I don't know,' I say, but I feel so grateful to him that I add, 'I can try.'

'It's not like you've got gangrene,' he says, with an expansive gesture. 'Get a massage, take it easy. Sorted.'

Jubilantly, I cash the cheque that Marco gave me and treat myself to a lunch of dolmades and saganaki in Chapel Street before making my way to Seaford to see Dad. The other day, I had a childish compulsion to see him, but today I actually want his company. I have no children to tend, a little money in my pocket and fresh motivation to sort out my life. Whether my hands can be 'fixed' is doubtful, but I'm tired of my wordless vendetta with the past. It's time to put down my sword and shield, take off my sandals and wander there. We can talk and eat a bacon sandwich cooked on that ridiculous grill and drink beer together.

Having been given permission, memories present themselves like creatures needing affection. I find myself thinking fondly of the first bicycle my father made me from bits and pieces he collected. I'd held the spanner and kept the rusty frame still while he worked. He later painted it pale pink from a spray can.

There were shoulder-rides to the beach with my mother striding before us, her red sundress whipping around her legs; the three of us eating fish and chips from the wrapper and tossing the dregs to the gulls; the matter-of-fact way he cleaned the grazes on my legs with Dettol after my first serious bike accident. When I had nightmares about the kidnapper in *Chitty Chitty Bang Bang*, he comforted me.

'It was too scary,' he said, cuddling me after I tearfully explained myself. 'Shouldn't've taken ya. I'm sorry, love.'

When he held me, fear vanished: that was the essence of his fathering.

There were other memories, too. Occasionally I heard my mother crying and breaking things at night. I'd lie very quietly, squeezing my teddy bear. Once she shouted out, 'I just can't stand it,' and I heard Dad reply in a low voice, 'I know, Ellen.' That night, I peeked through the door and saw him holding her. She seemed to have collapsed on the floor, hammering her own chest with clenched fists. Even though I was very young, I could see he wasn't being mean to her. It was something to do with her feelings, something terrible and deep: a monster that didn't hide in the cupboard or under the bed but inside her own body.

When I arrive at my father's place, I think I've taken a wrong turn: the house isn't there. Even the street looks unfamiliar without it, but it's the right street and the right number. 'They've done it,' I say aloud, trying to make sense of the demolition site in front of me. 'They've pulled his house down.'

In shock, I get out of the car and walk over to where the house stood only a few days earlier. There's nothing left but rubble and the mangled remains of the old rose, its green stalk still growing like an obstinate miracle from the dust. Further along the block the concrete mixer has gone, either removed or pounded to this grey powder that's everywhere, sticking to me. I crouch and sift the ossuary particles with my fingers. My left arm pulses.

'Oh Dad,' I say under my breath, 'I miss you.'

Something yellow catches my eye. It's the flaking paint of a crushed cigarette tin. I snatch it up and force it open. Inside there's a section of rubber, a few dozen nuts and bolts, very bright and tiny, and an old pulley. I pour these things into my palm and the weird howl I made on Blodwyn's table rises up inside me. Out it comes, loud enough to summon a neighbour or two; a piteous, raw wail, harsh as ice cracking.

That night, I pull the sleeping bag out of the car boot and sleep on Seaford beach. Waves break over the sand and starlit foam ripples through the darkness. For dinner I eat a beef hamburger and almost gag on the meat; but I need something to earth me, something visceral and hard to digest, to preoccupy the physical body and ease the other sensations.

I roll up the picnic blanket and use it as a pillow, and dig myself a little hollow in the sand using my feet. Pulling the sleeping bag hood around my chin and looking into the sky, I wonder at the constant stars. Even knowing ourselves in our wreckage, something in our nature makes it impossible for us to emulate the penguin and his clean, simple life. He doesn't have to question the stars; he just lives by their rhythm, a chord set at his birth and repeated for him and his ancestors and descendents, in an infinite, harmonious logic.

Just weeks ago, I knew what I believed. Now everything is uncertain. Tom fell in love with his 'desert-tribe girl' who couldn't distinguish between splendour and filth but knew how to love. He's right; I am not her any more. These days I'm so ruthless at separating splendour from filth that I am somehow dismembered. It's not love I've forgotten, surely – there's such love pouring through me for the children, for Tom, my father. But how do I *re*-member myself? So much depends upon it. My head spins, and I feel dizzy with the puzzle of it.

Pain wakes me before dawn. My ribs ache, no doubt from sleeping awkwardly on the sand. Breathing hurts. The pain in my hands and arms has receded to a diffuse backdrop for this new pain, bright and sharp. Still and scared, scoured by the stiff sea breeze, I'm astonished by the knife crossing from my right side into my chest. Every inhalation seems to drive the knife-tip into my lungs. I'm too scared to sit up, too scared to do anything but breathe.

Somehow I must have fallen asleep again because the sun has risen. Sand whips into my eyes. Tom was with me in my dreams. Long and lean, with a dim sheen to him, in our bed at home with the curtains billowing.

Cautiously, I shift and raise my neck slightly. The pain roars back.

Just need to get myself to Blodwyn.

Through the pain and the glare of the sun I see a penguin bobbing towards me. Not a metaphor or a vision: a real, live, actual penguin, peering at me from the edge of my burrow. Behind it a pair of human legs: sturdy, muscular, with wrinkly knees covered in ginger hair.

'What's up, skinny?' says Dad, standing over me. 'Y'look like an old woman.'

'Good to see you too, Dad,' I grunt. 'It's my back.'

Wisely, he doesn't try to lift me up. He extends a hand which I grip, pulling myself to my feet. The sleeping bag drops.

'How did you know I was here?'

'One of m'mates at the pub said he saw you crying at the old place. My baby wailing for her daddy.' He's teasing me but he can't disguise the genuine delight in his voice. 'So I rang your house and got Tom. Then this morning, I found your car.'

'I've gotta go,' I say. 'Just help me to the car.'

'But weren'tcha looking for me?'

'I was. But now my back's that crook...'

He picks up the sleeping bag and we shuffle over the sand, followed by the penguin. I don't ask him about the penguin, I know exactly what's happened: he likes it, so he's keeping it. He's very careful how he holds me. There's always a hint of beer and onions about him, even when he's just showered and his skin is damp, like it is now. Beer, onions and Imperial Leather. When we get to the car, he finds the keys in my jeans pocket and opens the door. His ute's alongside, the back covered with a tarpaulin; I wonder if a tall lump is my sculpture.

'Can ya drive?'

'I hope so.'

I wonder how much he and Tom said on the phone. There's no point asking; my father's too intractable to give me any useful information. He'd just tease me, hearing the need in my voice. I edge myself into the driver's seat, all at once exhausted by the reality of him.

'You must be hungry,' Dad says.

'There's a picnic basket in the back.'

He rummages around and presents me with a cheese sandwich and a bottle of water.

'Have one,' I say.

He gets in the other side, leaving the door open to watch over the penguin. We eat in silence. I feel a little better. My neck releases slightly, though not enough to turn around. I'll have to trust the mirror.

'You want to talk about Tom?' asks my father.

'No,' I reply.

'Life's roughing y'up a bit right now,' he says. 'Don't be scared of it. Learn how tough you *really* are when you're not pretending to be tough.'

He takes one of my sore hands in his own, lending me his warmth. He's always been a furnace as I am a furnace; we've funnelled our passion into odd, mostly manageable shapes because you can't be with others when you're nothing but a live ribbon of passion. And now my hands are cold and paralysed, and I don't understand them.

Dad turns the wrist over and strums the veins and tendons with his thumb. 'Jesus Christ,' he says. 'The strings in there are wound that tight they're gonna snap.'

Getting myself to Blodwyn wasn't easy. I leaned over the steering wheel so my hands and forearms shared the work, using my elbows to indicate. I tried to get into the freeway's left-hand lane. A car surged into my blind spot. What was he doing? I turned my head. Something ripped between my ribs and neck, and I screamed.

At Blodwyn's, tulips and butterflies make everything bizarrely pretty and homely. Bees and jasmine sweeten the air with wing-glints and fragrance and buzzing. Almost there. Just a few more minutes. Unshowered, unbrushed and bent over like a crone, I finally make it to the waiting room. The receptionist leaps out of her chair to half-catch me.

'I don't have an appointment,' I gasp.

'Just come this way.'

There's the subtle scent of pure beeswax and twigs burning in the fireplace. I am helped to the bench. Blodwyn leans over me, touching my back.

'It's time to let go,' she says.

So I tell her.

Tom and I stood by the gate and stared at the darkness of my parents' house. It was only ten o'clock and I expected to find them watching television in the front living room, the pale glow flickering over the sill. But not a single light gleamed anywhere. There was usually at least a porch-light left on for me.

'They must be in bed,' Tom murmured, his beer breath soft on my face.

By the front door a heavy-headed sunflower drooped over its stake. I licked sweat off my lip and turned the key in the lock. The door swung open silently.

The first thing I felt was a blast of cold air. The air conditioner was running at full-tilt. I shivered, rubbing at my arms. It was so unlike them to forget to turn it off. Tom sniffed, and reached for my hand.

'Is that vanilla?' he asked.

I didn't answer. My mother sometimes used vanilla when she cleaned the fridge. But it never smelled as strong as this.

I switched on the light and turned off the air conditioner. The motor ground to a halt. How clean the place was! Scrubbed and dusted and vacuumed. It was more than clean; there was hardly anything in there. Just furniture and vases filled with garden flowers. All the clutter had gone. There was a row of green bags filled with stuff along the wall. I undid the knot of one and found old toys and books and ornaments.

I hurried back into the hallway and opened the door to my parents' bedroom. The doona was stretched so tightly over the bed, there wasn't a single crease. My mother was tidy – but this was abnormal. That tight panel of cloth made my heart thump.

In the kitchen, too, everything was spotless – not a speck on the floor. All the paraphernalia from the fridge door was gone, even my wedding invitation. The grouting was white and clean. On the gleaming sink was a row of empty brown vanilla bottles and wine bottles and a sparkling wine glass upside down. I counted. Seven vanilla bottles. Two wine bottles. *Dad never drinks wine and Mum never drinks*. The wall-clock ticked loudly. I wanted to run away.

'Mum?' I called, glancing worriedly at Tom.

We looked in the laundry and bathroom, leaving lights on behind us. In my bedroom the mannequin wearing my wedding dress startled me. That only left the sun room. I crept along the hallway, my mouth dry, my heart jumping. I flicked the switch and the cruel fluorescence illuminated everything.

There was a smashed wine bottle on the floor next to where my mother crouched, rocking. She was wearing a worn black bra and a floral skirt pulled over her knees. There was a knife in one hand. From the side I saw cuts on her stomach. She looked strangely small and thin.

'Mum?'

'No, no, no,' she murmured, not looking at me. Her dark hair was whorled and matted. There was a sickly sheen to her pale skin and she smelt of blood and sweat. I looked across at Tom's shocked face – he'd never seen her like this.

'We'd better call an ambulance,' he mumbled.

'No,' I said. 'Dad never does. No ambulance, no police. They can't help.'

Tom took a deep breath, still staring. Then he crouched down beside her.

'I wouldn't,' I warned him.

'Let me take that knife, Ellen,' he said, quietly.

'No,' said my mother, shrinking from him. Her eyes were smeared with shiny mascara. She drew her knees closer to her chest.

'It's okay, Ellen,' Tom said, bending closer and reaching for the knife.

'No!' she shrieked, suddenly thrashing her arms about like a marionette. She lunged at Tom, and the knife gashed deep into his cheek. He slumped back with a grunt, clapping a hand against the flap of gaping flesh. I screamed.

'Mum! No – oh God! What have you done?'

She dropped the knife and stared at Tom. Blood dripped through his fingers – *too much blood*. I rushed to him, my gut churning. His pupils dilated frighteningly.

'Tom! Are you all right?'

He nodded slowly, but didn't move.

'We've got to get that stitched up,' I said, trying not to panic. 'Right now. Can you get up?'

'But what about Ellen?' he stammered. His blood was beginning to stain the floor. I turned to Mum.

'Come on,' I said, clasping her cold, clammy hand in mine. 'You need to come with me.'

'No,' she said, shaking me off. We tussled for a moment, hopelessly. I began to cry.

'Mum, *please*! Tom needs to go to hospital.'

She grew very still then, her eyes fixing on mine with pale intensity. And from her mouth came a strangled, awful sound. 'Rachel,' she cried, reaching for me now. 'I'm so sorry. I'm sorry. I ... I don't know what I was doing.'

'It's okay,' I said. 'Everything will be okay. But I need you to come with me now – I need to take Tom to hospital.'

'No,' she said, firmly. 'I can't come. Look at me – I need to get myself cleaned up.'

'I'm not leaving you.'

'Just go,' she cried. 'I'll only slow you down.' And as she said it, I knew she was right. The hospital was ten minutes away. 'Please hurry, Rachel. I'll never forgive myself.'

'Okay,' I said, uneasily. 'But I'm coming back for you.'

On the way to the hospital, Tom was conscious but dazed in the passenger seat. When we arrived, we were told there would be a two-hour wait – but Tom, the nurse informed us, would be made a priority. She handed me a wad of cotton for his cheek.

'I'll be all right,' he muttered. 'Really. You should get back to your Mum.'

'I don't want to leave you.'

'I'll be fine,' he said. 'Just go.'

I drove back to the house as fast as I could. This time, lights blazed in every window. Dad's ute was back. I dashed up the front steps, dimly aware of two different sirens in the distance: ambulance and police. I paused and turned. When I saw my father in a huddled ball on the front lawn, I almost lost control of my bladder. Steeling myself for what I might see, I entered the glaring house.

Blodwyn hands me a glass of water. She's a miracle worker; the pain in my back is almost gone. I can walk and breathe. Move my head from side to side. Even my arms feel easier. The water quenches my raw throat. I look up to find her face calm and full of sympathy.

What I couldn't express to her was the muteness that

took hold of me afterwards, thickening in my mouth like a wad of cotton wool, spreading its dullness through me.

Tom had wanted to put off the wedding.

'Why?' I asked.

He looked at me with incomprehension. 'We have to *tell* people.'

'She's dead. That's all anyone ever needs to know.'

'I still think…'

'Waiting won't change what's happened.'

I was efficient. I rang everybody and said the wedding was going ahead. I made the final arrangements for catering and music and stapled the programs by myself. We drove to Shellhorn mostly in silence with my wedding dress poking out of a garbage bag on the back seat.

'You're so brave,' one of Tom's sisters said to me at the time. 'I just can't believe your ability to cope.'

Blodwyn is watching me without judgment. She wanders around the bench, gazing towards the light at the window. 'You know, Rachel,' she murmurs. 'When the handless maiden becomes a queen, the king has a pair of silver hands made for her. They may be cold and hard but they are functional and beautiful. Above all, they disguise the absence of true hands, true courage, true strength. These silver hands so precious to you, the *I don't need help* hands – they're the hands you must now give up.' She smiles, and shrugs. 'Come and see me tomorrow. We don't want everything seizing up.'

Hands, muscles, fingers, skin. Arms, elbows, blood and bone. Cooking, washing, sewing, scrubbing. Lifting: children, wet clothes, groceries. Sculpting clay, kneading bread. And somewhere, in all this, is the force of life. A pressure that makes you well turned, well shaped, like the clay on my workbench. A pressure exerted by the needs of Joseph and Opal, who are innocent in all of this, even if I am not.

While Tom is away, I see a herbalist, a masseur and a doctor. But the person who helps me most is Blodwyn. To her I confess my deep shame: that I had chosen Tom over my mother, and in so doing I failed to save her.

'That's a heavy weight on Tom,' Blodwyn says.

'But I've never said that to him. I'm only beginning to see it myself.'

'Unspoken things have as much life as the spoken ones. Sometimes more,' replies Blodwyn. 'If your mother was here now, what would you say to her?'

A week before her death, I found my mother in my bedroom hanging a crystal necklace over my wedding dress on the mannequin. For weeks I had been putting veils and flowers and jewels against the cool white garment to see what looked best, wishing my mother didn't seem so depressed, wishing she'd join me. I watched as her fingers touched the fabric with such gentleness it was almost reverence. She turned towards me. On her face was an expression I had rarely – if ever – seen. Tenderness.

Behind my closed eyes, it is this expression that comes to me, with all the force of bittersweet memory.

'I'm sorry,' I whisper.

'And what does she say?'

There seem to be two realities around me. There is the physicality of the room, and the sounds from a distance – traffic, birds, breeze in the leaves and the current of the Yarra gushing beyond the garden. Behind Blodwyn a soft, green patch of daylight plays over the curtains.

In life, my mother wasn't affectionate. Her love was in the hours of work she did for me, like little scenes painted on children's blocks, etched in my memory, the same work I do now. She loved me. She's not angry with me. But that's not what she's saying. Another statement is forming in my mind.

I look up at Blodwyn, perplexed. 'She says, "true courage is in feeling".'

The summer morning is dense with the sound of cicadas. Geraniums bloom in wooden crates fixed to the windows. I savour their red joy, while summer bleaches the grasses and leaves outside. Tom is returning in three days; the children are yearning to see him. I am, too – though his emails and postcards have been very casual – and I'm doing my best not to hope for too much.

I'm scraping hardened porridge from the bench with a butter knife when there's a shout from the front porch and a thump. Opal's fallen. Flying down the steps, I can tell by the quality of the crying there's nothing seriously wrong.

'It wasn't me,' says Joseph, his arms are folded and defiant. 'She thought she saw Daddy and she was leaning too far.'

Sure enough, there's someone standing by the gate, tall and dark. It isn't Tom, it's Paisley. And Walter.

Paisley gazes across the dry garden. I can't say I'm happy to see her. The two of us take in each other, while swathes of pale grass swish this way and that between us. She's waiting for me to give the word. The children take the decision out of my hands; Opal runs down the steps and across the garden, crying 'Walter! Walter!' and puts her arms around her little friend. Joseph follows. They each take a hand of Walter's and drag him towards the house.

'Look at my bug-catcher,' says Joseph. 'I caught a ladybird this morning.'

Paisley stays where she is until I call: 'Come on in. I'll make some coffee.'

She has baked gingerbread. She lays it on the bench and takes a step away. 'Don't worry,' I say. 'I'm not going to throw anything at you.'

'I deserve it,' she says. 'I saw my chance and just went for it. I've always had a thing for Tom.'

There's an awkward silence while I pour the coffee, rich and dark. I put the gingerbread on a plate, a golden-brown circle inlaid with glistening smarties.

Paisley's staring at a tall white figure at the edge of the bench. 'That's not clay, is it?'

'No,' I say, 'It's wax – easier on the hands.'

'They're still bad?'

'Getting better.'

We sit at our old places by the little table on the porch. The old camaraderie is gone and the conversation is stilted, though we do laugh about that crazy night when I threw the stone. It's all still a little too raw, too near. Eventually, I say, 'Do you still want him?'

An involuntary grimace ripples through her lips and cheeks. 'It doesn't matter how I feel,' she says. 'He's not free.'

'What do you mean?'

'He comes with you attached. Even if you don't get back together. Anyway, I'm seeing someone now and I really like him. It might go somewhere. And I thought – you should know that.'

Sweet potatoes are roasting in the oven and gravy simmers on the stove. The table is covered with a cloth that I ironed last night – testing the new strength in my hands – and set with plates and twinkling glassware. Joseph has put a piece of polished rock by each plate and Opal a daisy. The daisies are wilting. My father carves a massive turkey. He's even made some kind of stuffing for it, with breadcrumbs and currants and spices.

We've been arguing about the penguin, presently splashing in the wading pool with the children in the front garden, waiting for Tom.

'Did you lie to me about the job in Cowes?' I say.

'Nup.'

'Why didn't you give him back then?'

'His mates weren't there,' he says. 'Too lonely for him.'

'I'm sure it's illegal to keep a penguin.'

'He likes me,' he says. 'Good distraction for the kids.'

Suppressing a smile, I shake my head at him as I fill the steamer with chopped beans and broccoli.

'You're a stubborn old bastard.'

'Takes one to know one,' he counters, prodding the turkey with a fork.

'No one's going to eat all that turkey, by the way.'

'Everyone will eat it,' my father replies, swigging his beer ceremonially. 'Except you.'

There's a great commotion when Tom arrives in a taxi. Through the window I watch him kneel and receive the children, who press themselves against him lovingly. There's luggage and presents strewn through the grass. Opal's laughing and Joseph pushes his cheek against Tom's, grinning. My father goes out to help him with his luggage. If Tom's surprised to see him it doesn't show. They shake hands. The warmth of his greeting carries up to the window:

'G'day mate.'

Tom turns, looking for me, and sees me through the glass. That dear face!

From there he can't see the new life in my hands. Nor can I make him see that when they do ache, it's the old silveriness reminding me to stay true to who I am. Smiling, Tom waves his hand and I raise mine in return.

SLOW TO LEARN

No one tells you what happens to time when you get old. Just like no one says what giving birth is really like, or that your mind and your heart never play any kind of sensible duet. No one ever tells you all the world you've been knitting unravels – and not just backwards but sideways and slantways and every other way, and you're forever scooping up the damned wool with your old, withering claws. Yes, they're withering. They're over ninety years old.

I once heard an intellectual say that when you look back over your life it flows like the plot of a novel. One decision leads to another, all making sense in the end. Well, I take issue with him over that. I bet they don't pat him consolingly yet. It might look like a plot when you're seventy. But when you get to my age, all the wool's undone and even as you knit it up, it still unrolls by colour, by pattern, strand by strand.

Like when there was a knock at our door late one night. It was more of a hammering than a knock; it had to be, to be heard over the heavy rain.

'Shipton! Ship! There's someone at the door,' I yelled.

Shipton was snoring like a train on his camping bed in the dining room. I knew the bastard wouldn't wake up. We were in our sixties by then and we thought we were old, we thought there was no hope for us; we'd more or less given up speech.

I reached for the mallet, stowed under the bed in case burglars tried their luck through my open window. The hammering came again, and with trembling fingers I switched on the lamp. Suddenly, a rain-wet face appeared at the window and I swung the mallet high in the air, ready to strike.

'For God's sake Mum, put that thing down! Don't you know your own bloody son?'

Well, I knew and I didn't – two things were happening at once. It was survival and motherhood, one instinct washing over another, raising the weapon while recognising my baby's face. Bill's eyes, blue chips in sun-browned cheeks, were unmistakable.

'Lucky I put the light on, or you might've been dead goods,' I told him, kicking the mallet under the bed.

Bill was no baby then, as soft-hearted as his sister Violet, but still getting into scrapes at thirty. When he was a boy, he made money by selling old newspapers to businessmen catching the train. One man missed the train to chase him the length of Chelsea station, but Bill kept his shilling, don't worry. He leapt off the platform and raced over the tracks, nimble as a billy goat. Another time I found camels in our backyard that Bill had brought home from the visiting circus. He was a rascal but he wasn't hard with it. Not hard enough.

I opened the door and saw Bill had Stevie in one arm and a hand on Cynthia's shoulder. Their hair dripped and their skin shone, wet and soft, under the porch light. Bill often turned up after a row, but to have the children with him — well, I knew this was serious. This was trouble.

That's one strand of things, and there are a few others like that. Like that summer's day when my grandfather dived into the wreck. I was staying with my grandparents in Queenscliff; my father had walked out on us. My grandfather was a deep-sea diver. Rich people in Melbourne employed him to find their treasures when ships were wrecked coming into Port Phillip Bay. He wore a suit sewn with ha'pennies, a twelve-bolt helmet with three layers of glass and diving boots heavy enough to walk the ocean floor.

There were two kinds of wreckage from these ships. Some – like the rolls of tweed fabric – washed up on the shore. (Locals hung the tweed in oilcloth bags under the pier to dry. For years we wore tweed and the hotels had tweed tablecloths, even napkins.) The rest stayed trapped in the ship and some of it was worth enough to risk the dive. Diving was perilous in those days. Crowds gathered on the pier to watch my grandfather's descent but my grandmother always forbade me to join them.

'It's not for children, Mavis,' Grandmother would say.

So I'd wait on the beach, gathering periwinkles and picturing my grandfather striding the sea beds, leaning forward into the water a little, carefully keeping his lifeline tangle-free. I yearned to be weighted with ha'pennies and walking beside him in that beautiful world, dark and softly green, with coral and kelp billowing from the sandy bottom and colourful fish swimming through the ship's broken hull.

When he found the treasure he gave three tugs on the line. Another line was lowered and he fastened the goods to the hook, and men would hoist it to the surface, reclaiming from the deep what belonged to the daylight.

That morning I heard a terrible shout. My stomach lurched, and brackish periwinkles stung the back of my tongue. On the boat I could see men rapidly hauling ropes, and I ran towards the pier where people were leaning over the railings and yelling. My grandmother saw me and cried '*Go back!*', with a face like a gargoyle, and I stumbled over on the sand, my tears drenching my cheeks with a child's immediate grief. I hugged my knees and rocked, saying *Grandfather* over and over.

The noise from the pier was deafening. With blurred sight I looked across to the boat and saw men waving. I didn't understand. Everyone was cheering! And then I saw my grandfather in his shining helmet rising, a traveller from another kingdom, and knew life would go on as before.

'Look at you Cynthia, you're soaked through,' I said, pulling the girl into the lounge room and switching on the electric heater.

Bill was talking. 'Charmaine'd locked the kids up and gone out. She knew I'd be late.'

Bill was a factory foreman and worked all hours. His sopping shirt clung to his muscular soldier's body. He and Charmaine had both been in the army and she made Bill marry her so she could leave. She couldn't take the discipline.

'Cynthia was banging her head on the headboard.'

There was a pink welt on the child's forehead. I marched into the dining room where Shipton slept on a camping bed, grabbed his shoulders and shook him.

'Get up,' I said, turning away from his groggy, bewildered expression.

Out came the blankets and towels. I lit the gas stove and set the kettle to boil; I raked around for dry clothes in my bedroom drawers. Bill followed me.

'The neighbours were trying to open the door,' he went on. 'I had to pick the lock. She *took the key*, Mum. She was over the back fence, with that bloody shopkeeper. I yelled out to her. I said, "I'm taking the kids to Mum's." She said, "Don't take Stevie. You can take Cynthia but don't take Stevie."'

'She's a little bitch and no mistake,' I said, heading back to the lounge room where Cynthia shivered by the fire. She was six, a heavy block of a child, with hair like white sunshine falling to her waist. She had her father's eyes, so pretty with pale silver lashes, but something wasn't right. Those eyes had a sort of milky look to them.

'Arms up,' I said, peeling away the wet nightie. I rubbed the child dry, dressed her in one of my own flannelette nighties, and wrapped her firmly in a blanket.

Poor little thing. Paying the price for those pills Charmaine took when she was pregnant, that's what I reckon. Little white pills in a jewelled pillbox, yellow ones in a cigarette tin. Valium, purple hearts. God knows where she got the purple hearts from; you couldn't get them from a pharmacist. Maybe a truckie boyfriend.

'Stevie needs a hot bath,' I said, and Bill handed over the scruffy bundle of toddler.

'No barf, no barf!' Stevie bawled, tears rolling down his cheeks. The whistle on the kettle started singing.

'What the bloody hell's going on?' shouted Shipton. 'Shut up. Can't sleep.'

'Get *up*, you lazy sod! And stop your swearing. The kids are here.' Back in the lounge I handed Stevie to Bill. 'Just wrap him in a blanket and we'll spread his pyjamas on the heater,' I said.

I made three mugs of strong, sugary black tea, the way we all liked it. Shipton emerged, wrestling with his dressing-gown, his blue eyes crackling like the gas flame. He was still handsome, his black hair lightly splashed with silver, his tanned skin ruddy on his cheeks.

Bill had slumped in an armchair with Stevie wrapped up on his lap. Cynthia was asleep. Rain poured noisily off the gutters outside. I could see new wrinkles of exhaustion on Bill. He'd been a beautiful boy: cheeky and wild and loving. He didn't have his father's chiselled jaw. He was softer. More gullible, certainly, working hard to pay off Charmaine's debts. Shipton would never have married someone who was forever lay-bying at Myer and forgetting. Silly as a bat, she was. Cunning though – she used her fishnet-lipstick-silk-pants beauty to seduce my son.

'Give Bill your bed and come in with me,' I said to Shipton, who was staring morosely at the tea leaves in his mug. He grunted, tapped the ash from his smoke and missed the ashtray.

'Aw, c'mon Dad. Won't do you any harm, if you know what I mean,' teased Bill with a flash of his old self, but neither Shipton nor I cracked a smile.

Twenty years before the day Bill and the children arrived on our doorstep, ten-year-old Bill had brought home the camels. I wasn't there to manage him; I was in hospital after fainting in the city.

I loved getting dressed up to go to town. In the days before jeans and T-shirts you put on a hat and gloves, and men still doffed their hats at women; that is, men who were gentlemen.

Most of the men in my family weren't gentlemen. I was always breaking my heart over them: my husband, my son, my father. For a while it seemed like my heart was always breaking but just when you think your heart is broken and the job's done, it starts breaking all over again. I must have said something like this to my daughter Violet one time because she sent me a beautiful poem, handwritten on a postcard. It was about the heart and written by Edna St Somebody. She was the only person to ever guess I might like a poem.

The one true gentleman I'd known was my other grandfather, who dropped my ratbag father from his will. (Dad cut up rough about it for years but I got three shillings and sixpence weekly for my keep till I turned eighteen.) I met that grandfather when I was four, in an unfamiliar courtyard – his, I suppose. Never had I seen anyone smoke a pipe so slowly. Together we watched the smoke dissolving into the sunlight as though there was nothing else to do in the world.

So anyway, that day I walked through the Block Arcade, stripping off my hot gloves when I reached Bourke Street to look at the Christmas display in the Myer windows. The baby Jesus was made from wax that year, tinted delicately in the style of the time, with rosy cheeks and golden curls. There was a fragile subtlety in his features that went beyond prettiness. Violet was born on Christmas day, and I felt a proprietary interest in all nativity babies.

When I felt an odd tremble through my legs, I knew I shouldn't have come. I dabbed at the sweat on my lip with a hanky. Trams shunted behind me. Hot gusts of wind flapped at my ankles. I straightened up, ignoring the sharp twinge in my belly, and thought of Shipton.

Shipton was no gentleman. He had beautiful manners in public and he was a good dancer, not that he ever took me dancing. Dancing would interfere with his nap. But he never lifted a finger to help me; he wouldn't even hold the babies while I did the dishes. He'd just watch while I struggled with a wailing infant, hot suds and congealed gravy, resting his dirty boots on the table. Well, I wasn't having any more children to him.

I swayed and steadied myself on the window, leaving sweaty streaks on the glass. I'd suspected a pregnancy for a few weeks and the day before had taken measures to get rid of it. Bill was ten, Violet was nearly twenty. No way was I returning to the backbreaking work of babies. No bloody way.

The first time I saw Shipton was in my mother's tiny kitchen in Port Melbourne. Shipton was the new boarder: a sailor from the merchant navy who'd jumped ship. Swinging in through the side door, I nearly fell over him and backed away hurriedly, staring. I'd never seen such a handsome man in all my life. Wide shoulders, narrow hips, a face with tight brown skin like polished oak. And his eyes! Satiny and the same greenish-blue as paua shell. His presence was so powerful I felt like I'd walked into a spell. A silly giggle burst from me. At first it was just a nervous giggle but then he joined me in a fit of laughing and I had to grab the sink, bent double.

Six weeks later we were married. No one pays for the milk if you give it out for free. Once you're married, though, it's there for the taking – and the consequences, too. That's the deal.

I would have keeled over outside Myer that day if the saleswoman hadn't come to help me, carrying a ream of brown paper over her arm. Why the brown paper, I wondered.

'I'll call a doctor,' she said kindly.

Something moving on the pavement caught my eye, a dark skirt spreading below me. Coming out of me. Blood.

'Where are you?' Shipton's voice was cantankerous over the phone. He had no idea I'd been pregnant. It was twins, I was sure of it. He had no idea about the syringe, the hot water, the antiseptic.

'I'm in the hospital. I've got to have a curette.'

'A *what*?'

'A curette! Something to clean me out.'

'But who's going to make my tea?'

I hung up on him. It doesn't sound much but the act of putting the receiver down changed our marriage forever. I lay back on the pillow without remorse and thought about that poem Violet had sent me.

When I finally got home I found Bill playing with camels in the garden, pleased as punch with himself. Three huge things, golden and scraggy, with leathery noses and kneecaps and smelling of fur and sweat.

When Bill brought his children through the rain that night, he said it would only be for a few days. But for the but that, of course, was nonsense. He had to work. For the next eight years, Stevie and Cynthia slept on mattresses on the floor in my bedroom. Shipton stayed in the dining room and Bill made another bed there that he packed up each morning.

My new dining suite with upholstered seats had to go.

So my life began all over again. I took Cynthia to all her appointments and enrolled her at the special school in Mordialloc. We went everywhere by train; I never learnt to drive. Sometimes I took the children to the beach to play. No one had books or played instruments but we listened to the new pop music on the radio. I liked the Beatles. The children loved to hear stories of how naughty their father was as a boy, especially the story of the camels. We watched *The Brady Bunch*, *I Dream of Jeannie* and *My Three Sons*; and my hands were never still, making all their clothes, knitting, crocheting, sewing, fingers flying, cigarettes burning at my lips.

Late one night, Charmaine came looking for her children, rattling on the front door and calling:

'William, William, it's your *wife*.'

Stevie whined. I pulled him into bed and shushed him. Bill creaked along the hallway and opened the front door.

'Where are my children, Bill?'

'Mum says you're not to come in here.'

There was a bit of pushing and shoving. The front door banged against the wall.

Cynthia whispered, 'That's my mum.'

'Yes, pet.'

'She didn't want me – she wanted Stevie.'

I was surprised the girl knew that, and hearing her say it pushed sharp in my throat.

The stone wall of grandfather's courtyard was covered in wisteria. He wore a smoking cap, an Oriental-looking thing, red with a tassel. The scents of wisteria and smoke wove together, a fragrant braid of indigo and violet. Beside him I felt safe and calm. A voice called from inside.

'Come away, Mavis, don't bother your grandfather.'

My grandfather called back, 'Leave the little girl alone', and I kept still as still could be, my heart beating with pride at being wanted by this silent, respectable man who said so decisively: 'She's staying with me.'

I would have, too. Given the choice.

Bill eventually moved out with the kids, to a bungalow in our backyard. Sometimes his wife showed up and there was strife – slammed doors and hysterical weeping. Cynthia reported events from the window while I knitted. Shipton watched television, driving us mad by crunching relentlessly on barley sugar. Age was wrapping him in its deathly shawl and he seemed very far away.

The children were hard work, but whenever I felt like complaining I remembered the two I'd forced from my body and I tried to bear it. Stevie got through school, and once I'd finished with Cynthia she could read a train timetable and manage a bank account.

'A woman learns to think things out with her own mind, to get by,' I told Cynthia. 'No one told *me* anything, not even the facts of life.'

She looked at me blankly when I told her that the first time I was in labour with her Aunty Violet I didn't know where the baby would come out. The Salvos were singing Christmas carols outside the hospital while I was wondering if the doctor would cut open the little crease in my tummy. The sheets were bundled and wet with my sweat. The sun flayed me through the window.

Beautiful Violet, actress and acrobat, with a supple golden body and a heart as soft as butter. Violet, who posted me a poem, born to the Salvos bellowing 'Good Christian Men Rejoice'. When her head crowned she shocked the living daylights out of me.

'If you're so bloody joyful,' I raged at those Salvos, 'why don't you come in here and have a go at this?'

We laughed about that, Cynthia and I.

When Shipton died, I realised the conversation I'd been decades waiting for was never going to happen. I hung up on him, he died forty years later and we didn't say much in-between. The day after his funeral, Cynthia and I walked along the beach. The cold sand felt good under my feet.

I gazed out to the ocean, remembering how when I was a little girl, I ate raw periwinkles to stave off hunger, pulling their squishy, salty bodies straight from the shells into my mouth. And while I haven't been hungry in that violent, physical way since the Depression, I've been hungry in a different way – wide and nameless.

Two weeks before he died, Shipton asked Stevie to go to the milk bar for barley sugar. 'Sure, Pop,' said Stevie, taking the money and winking at me. 'Back soon.'

Stevie returned with marshmallows. He handed them over solemnly. How we laughed at Shipton's dumbfounded expression as he pulled the quiet, powdery sweets from the plastic! He couldn't see the joke and I felt cross. How could he let himself get old so wilfully, even lose his sense of humour? But when he died I felt terrible about it. The poor bastard *was* old; he was about to shuffle off, and all he wanted was a bit of barley sugar.

We'd had such fun once. He'd begged for cakes and my first cakes were hard as rocks. When he got home from work he dug them out of the garden and nailed them to the wall. I was offended. Then I saw his wicked grin and we both laughed so hard tears streamed from our eyes. He *had* loved me. He must have. A bit.

After the beach, Cynthia and I went to the Chelsea Cake Kitchen, a hot-pink establishment with its name alight in swirling neon above the door and the radio tuned to 3AW talkback. The formica tables were packed with council workers and mothers in tracksuits with plastic bags of groceries. We ordered two vanilla slices, tea and a spider.

We pulled out our knitting bags to make baby blankets for a neighbour and Violet's old postcard drifted onto my lap. I re-read the familiar words. I'd always liked the first *pity me not* lines but this time my eyes focused on the last two:

> *Pity me that the heart is slow to learn*
> *What the swift mind beholds at every turn*

I blinked back tears. My heart still hasn't learned. Is that what I've been trying to pull together, all this time?

'Nan, tell about Dad and the camels,' said Cynthia, wanting my tears gone.

'I don't feel like that story, pet.'

'Please Nan. Please.'

'Well, okay. When your dad was little a circus set up in the paddocks over the road. Ooh, your dad chatted with them all, always trying to get something for nothing. The camel trainer said, "anyone who wants to look after these camels can come to the circus every night for free!" So Bill, quick as a wink, put up his hand.

'When I got home there they were, three camels taller than the back fence – and there was your dad, making them stand up and sit down, pretending he was a circus trainer.

'I told him off but I didn't really mind. They lived with us for a week and were ever so well behaved. The place was chock-full of blackberries and the camels ate them all. Those thorny blackberries went down as easily as sponge cake and a cup of tea.'

'One hump or two?' said Cynthia, laughing like a child of six, probably the age she was when she first heard the joke.

'Yes dear, that's right,' I smiled but I was tired – so tired. Life just keeps *going*. And *repeating*. We walked home and Cynthia made sweet-and-sour Chinese food with too much sugar. We watched *Prisoner*, Bill came up from the bungalow for a cuppa, and we had a laugh about Charmaine wearing a kaftan at the funeral. She told Bill she'd become a white witch, and tried to put a spell on Cynthia to help her lose weight.

There would be one change, I decided. I'd pack up my knitting. I'd reel in every little skein of wool and put it neatly in the wicker chest beside my chair. For the first time in fifty years, I'd stop pulling all the strands together and let my hands lie idle.

That evening, after my hands had been still for a whole hour, my sleep was restless. I dreamed of myself as a young woman, wearing my grandfather's diving boots, standing on a beach. The boots weighed so much it hurt to move. Her brow was creased with pain. *You are supposed to jump from a boat, not wade in from the shore*, I wanted to tell the young woman as she walked resolutely into the waves. Under the water were the bodies from the shipwrecks, flying in green washes of light. I searched the faces. One of them would be Shipton's. I was looking for it.

THE EASTER HARE

Friday.

For two dusks, the body hangs from a rope coiled over a branch. Under moonlight, like a stone, the wind ruffling the leaves around it, the grasses below it. Dew gathers and dissipates over the bluish skin. Flies settle undisturbed on the lips and eyelids and ears. Bellbirds make their one-note, haunting chimes.

The children walk along the track with their father, Mark. 'Can't catch me Dad! I'm faster than you!' yells Alice, suddenly darting ahead. Their mother, Stephanie, lags behind, enjoying the scents of the trees, the green swathes of moss interrupting the dusty bush grey. Toby, her son, pauses here and there, finding holes that might house wombats or gnomes. Stephanie enjoys the small crouch of him, his intent, wondering gaze. It's Easter Friday, the first day of a long weekend.

The cool morning evaporates and children shed woollen hats and jumpers. Stephanie folds them over her arms. Skinks scuttle over the rocks.

'Are we there yet, Dad?' calls Alice.

'Not yet.'

Close by, on a parallel track somewhere above them, a jogger thuds over the gravel. Stephanie hears him. He sweats in his long-sleeved top and smears a forearm over his brow. A mobile phone in his shorts' pocket smacks his thigh rhythmically. It might ring at any moment; his wife is due any day. Her every cell seems pregnant. A glowing layer softly swells her fingers, her ankles, her neck: she is *infused* with child. The two of them have been busy preparing, painting the bedroom, stripping carpet, working extra shifts to pay for the cot and highchair.

When jogging, he imagines what it might be like to

hold his child for the first time. The baby skips across his mind like a stone skimming a river, and his heart skips with anxious joy.

'I'm boiling, Dad. I'm a boiled egg,' Alice declares, peeling away her T-shirt.

'Please can I go swimming? Please!'

It's more command than request. Mark constructs a makeshift platform from logs for Alice's descent. Alice removes her clothes. Shining like a pearl in the sunlight, she lowers her round and muscular child-body into the river. Toby watches, disinclined to follow her into the sparkling brown water.

Stephanie watches, quietly composing a story for her children around the Easter Hare. The crucifixion is too much. It is bloody and harsh. Then there's the darkness of Easter Saturday. The disconnection, the wilderness. The feeling of being locked out. She barely grasps it herself, even in fragment.

She can create something gentler for them. The traditional spring symbolism is a challenge in autumn, and the Easter bunny's cuteness has never been meaningful to her. The hare, however, has other possibilities. A hare has intelligence and courage. And they say that a hare protects its own, to the point of sacrificing itself.

Alice emerges. They discover that one of the logs placed in the water was a home for bull ants. Mark and the children begin a rescue operation, sliding another log under the floating creatures and drawing them back to the land. The sky fills with clouds, and where there was warmth comes coolness. Autumn: from bathing in the river at lunch time to baking by an open fire at night. Stephanie urges clothes back over Alice, secures the hatband under Toby's chin. They walk uphill, towards the jogger's track.

The jogger hurtles to a halt. Beyond him, not ten metres away, a dead body hangs from a gum tree. He wipes his brow, presses his fingers to his eyelids. The body is unbearably still. He drops his head, unwilling to look. His own, living body registers horror in increments: the skin, the stomach, the heart. For a moment he feels he might vomit. He reaches to his hip and draws out the mobile phone. It is silver, unnaturally bright in the muted landscape. Never has he felt more grateful for this tiny cold portal to another world.

He makes the call. Triple zero. Relays the message to the operator. He stands there for a while, perhaps fifteen minutes, waiting for the paramedics. He doesn't look at the corpse again. More than anything he would like to flee the sickly atmosphere created by the dead body, hanging so utterly still. Then he hears, not far behind him, children's voices.

Stephanie touches Mark's elbow. 'Look, what's that? There's something wrong with that man.'

The jogger is waving his hands, gesturing at them to stop.

'I'll go and see what's wrong,' says Mark.

The man runs towards Mark. The children *must not* see that hanged body. He doesn't care if he looks like a lunatic. He'll stop them seeing that corpse. The mother and the girl and boy are motionless, watching him. Their faces are alive and beautiful. The girl's eyes are a searing blue, her whole body a question.

'What is it, mate?' Mark says, placing a warm hand on his arm.

The jogger wonders if his legs will buckle. He steadies himself, looking upwards. The whorled, twisting shapes of the clouds look like corridors. *There's a word for what that looks like*, he thinks.

'A body. Hanging from a tree just over there. So you've got to stop the kids. Go back the other way,' he says, keeping his voice steady.

A volute? No. No, a vortex. Something seems to be coming unhinged in him, something that had been securely lodged.

Mark sees, over the man's shoulder, a white and red vehicle driving slowly along the track. The red lights flash but there is no siren. Stephanie takes hold of the children's hands and turns them around.

'Why is there an ambulance, Mummy?' Alice asks. 'Is that man sick?' They walk the long way back and tell a flustered story about a snake to explain their change of direction.

Back at home that night, Toby helps his father bring wood for the fire. They build it up, layering heavier wood over kindling and balled-up newspaper. Mark sharpens sticks for them to pierce marshmallows and toast them in the flames.

'Why did that man tell us there was a snake, Mum? Why did we have to go back the other way? asks Alice.

Stephanie thinks the story should have been more truthful, somehow. Alice senses it and presses for more satisfying answers, getting so distracted with the snake story that she burns her marshmallows.

'Sometimes it's better not to get in the way of a snake,' says Stephanie. 'Try to keep the marshmallows just above the fire, so they go a nice, soft brown. Are you going to toast one for your dad?'

'What else could we have told them?' Mark says under his breath, sinking into the couch beside her. 'How could we have explained it?'

'I wonder what happens now,' muses Stephanie. 'Do they go to the hospital or the morgue?'

'Who's going to the hospital?' demands Alice, from across the room.

Somewhere, someone is receiving terrible news. Perhaps the person who tended him when he was small and new and full of delight and hope. The one who washed him, fed him, sang to him. The mother.

Years ago, a friend she knew from university committed suicide. Joe was slight, bright-eyed, and loved to quote Noël Coward or Spike Milligan during tutorials. (*I thought I'd begin by reading a poem by Shakespeare but then I thought, why should I? He never reads any of mine.*) In his more serious moments he was a gifted essayist. His emotional intensity was intriguing; and he often told Stephanie crazy anecdotes from his weekends. Obviously there were things she couldn't know.

Why did he end it? Like a finger and a thumb pinching a candle flame, he snuffed his own light. She had wept about him for days, although she hadn't really known him. What was he facing that was worse than death itself? Suicide is acres of darkness. The more you pitch your spade into it, the more darkness you dig up.

Saturday.

Toby and Alice prepare a basket for the Easter Hare. They each polish an apple. Stephanie cuts a third apple to show them 'the star within' they read about in an Easter Hare story. The apple splits in two, revealing the star-shape around its nest of black seeds. In the story, the hare exchanges autumn apples for eggs, with 'the sun within' from on the other side of the earth, where it's spring.

Alice spreads a coloured cloth in the basket and they place the apples inside. They leave it on the back step. Stephanie gathers them to her, and they spend a few moments gazing into the night sky.

In the next suburb, Julie and George watch television, and Julie feels a clamping sensation in her lower belly. It is beginning. She says nothing to George for a while. She plaits her hair. They lie on the couch. George nestles his heavy head into the crook of her shoulder. He has been so tender over the past few days. He is ready. They are both ready.

George watches the television, intently. Now and then, he holds his wife's plait up to the lamp to examine the texture, the interweaving of gold and brown and red. Nothing he looks at cancels the image of the hanged man, which is permanently fixed in his mind. He hasn't told Julie. He won't let that horror touch the unborn one, even as a picture in Julie's imagination.

A powerful urge to protect was born in him the day Julie said she was pregnant; it has only grown stronger over the weeks and months. It almost knocked him over yesterday when he heard those little children coming towards the hanged man, their innocent eyes about to behold a tragedy.

The children's father had seen his distress and stepped to his aid with a comforting hand, a matter-of-fact voice. There was some essence of fatherliness there, something for him to step towards. When he was seven, his own dad had patted his shoulders and said: 'It's good to see they're growing broad, son.'

'That means I'll be strong,' George had replied.

'Yes, you'll be strong,' his father said. 'With plenty of room on your shoulders for people to cry on.'

George had often recalled this statement. When it flitted into his thoughts – while looking at his broad frame in the mirror, or carrying something heavy – he had dismissed it as a bit silly or sentimental. Now it seemed urgently true.

Alice and Toby have helped their mother weave long strips of dough into baskets and they can smell them baking in the oven. They are restless and excited. Stephanie lights a candle. She is very tired now, longing to sit quietly. She searches herself for a story.

'Tell, Mummy!' commands Alice, wriggling into bed.

'Is the Easter Hare coming tonight,' asks Toby.

The image of the hare arises in the Stephanie's mind. His long and beautiful ears are like ladles, scooping elusive sounds from the quietness of space. He looks at her, his paws on his chest, waiting patiently for the meanings she will cast over him.

'In a pretty town, on a pretty street, there's a row of cottages,' she begins, and the children's eyes shine with anticipation. 'By each front door are baskets filled with harvest apples. Not far away, the animals of the forest have gathered, staring across the fields at the village. The animals have heard a rumour that the Easter Hare is coming. They have never seen him.

"Where does he live?" asks the possum.

"He has no burrow," says the rabbit.

"Everywhere is his home," says the wombat. "Everywhere – or nowhere."

The animals decide to stay awake all night to see him. But one by one they fall asleep: the magpie, the possum, the wombat, the rabbit, the kookaburra. They snuggle together, and in the warmth of their bodies they fall into a deep, dreamy sleep. They wake at dawn. *Oh no, have they missed seeing him?* But there, in front of them, is the Easter Hare, tall and sturdy, with the sun shining behind him. He gazes down at the forest creatures. The hare's eyes are round and dark, full of a deep, loving kindness. In one bound, he is gone and as the sun rises over the village, the children find the rainbow eggs in their baskets and the animals hear their shouts of joy.'

Sunday.

Before dawn, after fifteen hours of labour, the baby is laid on Julie's bare skin. She is tiny and rosy. George is weeping. Julie lays one hand on his head and the other on the baby's. She isn't crying. She feels vast. After-echoes of pain shimmer through her body, and the tremendous relief at the clean sensation of pain's departure. She didn't resent it – how could there be no pain when your very physical body is a bridge between one world and another? She isn't even sleepy. The baby's face is tilted upwards. The delicate, fresh face sears itself into Julie; she knows it will be with her always.

Alice and Toby collect their treasures from the Easter Hare, hidden all over the garden. Their eyes are alight from the excitement of the hunt. Stephanie lays the bread baskets on the table and Alice and Toby put the eggs inside and light candles. Friends have come from up and down the street to eat eggs and play in the garden and to listen to another of Stephanie's stories.

In the afternoon, Stephanie drives by herself to the state park where they walked on Friday. This time she walks briskly along the jogger's track, searching for the place of the suicide. Feathery violet clouds drift across a sky as pale as milk. An earth-smelling autumn breeze wraps her small, compact shape. She comes to the place. There's no rope, no body; only the trace of it, a memory in the landscape. A strip of red and white tape flaps against the gum tree.

Stephanie kneels and draws out a small geranium from

her pocket. She places it at the foot of the tree, where its soft colour glows on the dust.

She allows herself to encounter the terror. Inwardly, she opens the door. What if this boy was her boy? The grief passing through her is more like nausea. The hair on her arms stands up. Her upper lip arches and she lets out a sob. Against her cheek comes a little rush of wind, as though a bird has swooped by, and in this she feels a definite sense of flight, of departure, as though a decision has been made somewhere.

Stephanie presses her fingertips, then her palms, onto the dusty earth either side of the flower. 'I didn't know you,' she says, 'but I hope you find your way.'

THE RINGWOOD MADONNA

'Watch how the gold leaf brings the icon to life,' the art teacher said in the final class. She gazed at the students with earnest eyes. 'Gold, fire and lightning are beautiful in themselves because they *are* light.'

For weeks Ula had been labouring on her icon of Mary, painstakingly tracing the image onto graphite paper and preparing her woodblock with six layers of gesso. She felt almost visceral relief when it came time to carve Mary into the gesso with a nail. She bent her llama-like neck over her woodblock, squinting and sucking in her cheeks. The precision required for icon painting distracted her from herself. She liked how the colours had fixed meanings – even the prototype itself was unchanged for over a thousand years. She liked certainty in things, too: black and white, right and wrong, no complex interpretations. It was probably why she'd become an accountant.

'Gold, fire and lightning *are* light,' Ula repeated to herself as she pressed the gold leaf onto burnt umber with steady hands, unaware of the flush spreading over her brow. She caressed the Madonna's timeless face, pleased that she'd captured something of the icon's unique expression; intuitive, solitary, compassionate.

On the train home she nursed the icon close as the suburbs streamed past her window: hideous billboards and fences covered in graffiti, a confused swirl of the grizzled, the graceful and the depraved.

'Gold, fire and lightning to the lot!' she thought, tightening her grip on Mary.

She didn't tell Mike the art classes had finished. She wanted to keep Thursday night as a window in the week free of her maternal concerns. She handed Mike the warm bottle for Tania and took off as normal, her painting kit slung over her shoulder. Except on this occasion she was in the grip of a plan, possibly an insane one. She'd spent nights fantasising about painting an icon of Mary some place where it couldn't be ignored. And now here she was, walking along railway tracks as night deepened.

She was determined to act before she could think herself out of it. Her headlamp shone on some of the brashest images splashed out of Ringwood. Black scrawls over a distorted depiction of Shrek. Genitalia. A silver-paint phrase: 'Aussie Transit Malisha.' Did they mean *militia*? A fat pink word saying 'Pigfucker'. Broken glass crunched under her Dunlop Volleys. The earth smelled like an unflushed toilet.

'The image comes out of dark to light,' Ula murmured, recalling the art teacher's words. Excitement, joy, even warmth burgeoned in her breast. She could put *words, gold, the magical efficacy of love. My act of rebellion, a drop of beauty, a site of defiance.* She sprayed a white space for Mary and wished birdsong or a train whistle would break the intimate quiet as she waited for it to dry. She unfolded a card table and laid out jars of paint and water. She tested the white square with her forefinger. Into burnt umber went the brush, and she painted an outline.

'Hey, what are you doing?' came a voice from the dark.

Ula yelped and lurched sideways, knocking over her paints. A Maglite beam moved across her face. Ula's breath came fast. She had no good excuse for being there.

When the light was lowered, Ula's headlamp illuminated an adolescent boy, perhaps seventeen, twirling the torchlight over the ground at her feet. Green and brown beer bottles glinted in the grass. He put a cigarette between his lips and lit it with a match, waiting for the flame to burn down to his fingers before tossing it to the ground.

'Do you – work here?' Ula asked lamely, her tongue loosening.

'What are you doing?'

'My own … graffiti,' she said, feeling ridiculous. She bent to retrieve her paint jars from under the card table, to cover her embarrassment. The boy watched. She squeezed out her brushes and packed them in her bag with a regretful glance at the hollow Mary glowering back at her.

'Doesn't look like graffiti.'

'No,' she said, 'I guess it doesn't.'

'I'm a tagger. Know what that is?'

The torchlight was making figure eights around her feet.

'Not really.'

'The *lowest of the low*.'

Ula didn't understand the emphasis of his words. Was he being sarcastic, funny or threatening? He sounded like he was quoting someone else.

'Is there any of your work here?' she asked.

The boy pointed at the Shrek. What had looked like a scrawl was actually an ornate D.

'What does D stand for?'

'Duke.'

'Is that your name?'

He gave her a condescending look.

'It's my *tag*.'

'Oh, I see. I think – I should go. '

Duke didn't answer as she folded the card table and walked away, stubbornly resisting an impulse to run. She didn't want him to think she was scared. The tracks curved before her like a river, rust-coloured, shineless. Glancing over her shoulder she saw the forlorn figure of Duke, no more than a child really, blowing smoke into the darkness.

When Tania was born, Ula felt there must be a mystical secret behind all of life. She was curvy, billowing, maternal. And forty-four. Love sustained her through the shock of hips opening like gates, stomach muscles parting like curtains, blood and vernix, soiled nappies, sleeplessness. And then, at some point, Ula succumbed to exhaustion. Her curves vanished too fast. Anxiety took hold. It started with scrambled eggs. Tania, only four months old, was looking hungrily at her scrambled eggs and Ula gave her a few spoonfuls. Only later, with the child drawing her knees to her chest and screaming, did Ula remember the Health Nurse saying '*no egg*'.

When she finally got her to sleep, Ula sank into a chair, picturing Tania's little pink mouth innocently receiving the egg and her fragile digestive track buckling with strong food. Now Ula often woke in dread, convinced she'd forgotten something crucial to Tania's wellbeing. Sometimes she felt waves of fear rushing up and down her body as she awaited Tania's cry for her midnight feed. When the cry finally came, her startled breasts would leak hotly.

'I don't know if I'm cut out for this,' Ula had told the Health Nurse at Tania's six-month check-up.

'None of us are,' she replied. 'You cut yourself out for it.'

The doctor gave her a script for anti-depressants. Ula thanked him but didn't see how they would help. She wanted to feel more, not less. Well – less anxiety, more love. There's no drug for that. She had the script filled and left the packet unopened by the kitchen sink. Instead, she drank some leftover Christmas sherry. *Just to warm me up a bit*, she told herself.

Another Thursday came and went. Ula hadn't the energy to go back to the unfinished Mary but she couldn't stop thinking about her, either. Despite the hot weather she felt cold and robotic, her heart like a gaudy red jewel in her chest. She wanted to thaw herself by Mary's gold. Her narrow, brain-bound fixation on Mary felt to her like a sociopath's understanding of a conscience. That she reminded herself of a sociopath was yet more cause for concern.

One afternoon she pushed the pram into the driveway and saw the hammock on the verandah bulging. She tightened her grip on the handle and glanced along the street. It was empty. There was no car parked in front of the house, so it couldn't be Mike, home early from work. He rarely came home early these days – who could blame him? He was likely to find the house upside down and Ula in tears.

Ula put the break on the pram. Tania's face was pink and blotchy and irritable. She was over-tired. *Don't cry. Keep quiet.* Ula climbed the steps, turning her phone over in her pocket, and saw it was Duke lying there, smoking.

'What – what are *you* doing here?' she said, her voice shrill.

'Wanted to see you,' said the boy.

'But how–?'

'Followed you that night.'

His voice was sullen, entirely unapologetic. Ula looked him over in the daylight: a long piece of black hair covering one eye, bad skin, tight jeans and Converse shoes. The one eye she could see was ringed with kohl. She wondered if he intended to look so cheap and camp.

'You gonna finish that chick you were painting?'

Ula sucked in her cheeks and chewed them for a moment. Tania started crying. She hurried down the steps to get her, returning to unlock the front door, holding her arm like a shield over the baby. Duke slid out of the hammock.

'That your kid?' he asked.

'Stay out here and I'll bring out a cup of tea.'

She didn't want Duke coming inside the house and seeing how she lived.

'I don't drink tea.'

'Beer?'

'Water.'

Ula dashed inside and put Tania in her cot, praying she'd go down easily. She brought out water and cake and a mug of sherry for herself. She took a slug and relished its sweet scald. Duke stretched his skinny legs under the outdoor table. He lifted his glass to drink and Ula noticed his dirty nails bitten to the quick.

'Why did you want to see me?' she asked.

'Don't you want me here?'

'You said – before – you wanted to see me.'

The boy shrugged.

'I don't remember.'

He drank his water. Pimples crusted his neck. With one eye blinking at her he ate the cake.

'Where do you live?'

'Here and there.'

'Are you homeless?'

'I can't go home because of my step-dad.'

'Did he hurt you?'

'Yeah.'

He spoke blandly, his eye never moving off her face. Ula wondered if he'd detached from his suffering in order to survive. A cynical voice was asking *is he just trying to get sympathy?* But – poor boy – what if it was true? *Something's gone wrong for him.* Silence clotted between them. A furtive glance at her watch told her it was five o'clock. Mike would be leaving work. Duke finished all the cake and lit another cigarette. Watching Ula, he again let the flame burn to his fingertips before dropping the match. She was about to tell him off when Duke said: 'I light fires.'

His lowered voice streaked through the silence like a demon, chilling the skin at her nape.

'You'd better go,' she said, standing up. 'My husband will be home soon.'

Duke grinned. 'Scared you,' he said.

Ula frowned. Shrugging defensively, Duke slouched down the stairs, and out through the front gate without looking back.

Ula read everything the Health Nurse gave her. Instructions on motherhood. She dreaded being left alone with Tania. What if she made a mistake? A baby wasn't like a tax return you could fill in correctly. Tania was chaotic and unpredictable, too small to leave anything to chance and somehow too big to comprehend.

March was hotter than February. Ula didn't see Duke again until she was shopping for a shirt for Mike in Eastland Shopping Centre, pushing the pram. Duke materialised in front of them, eyebrow cocked. He looked thin. Bruised crescents curved under his eyes.

'Hi,' he said.

How young and lonely he seemed. *Neglected*. Something rushed through her, a feeling not for herself but for him. Fellow feeling.

'You should look after yourself,' she said, and touched his arm.

A muscle twitched in his left cheek. 'You gonna finish her off?' He meant the Madonna.

'I don't know.'

'You should,' he said. He was *interested*. Or was he daring her?

'It's hard to get out.'

She gestured at Tania. The baby looked up at them both, smiling, eyes bright. She cooed at Duke as he turned and shuffled off. Tania babbled and pointed. Ula saw she wasn't so little any more. She was keenly alert, clear as a diamond, ready soon to get out of her pram and walk.

Ula scanned the crowd as she went down the escalator, expecting to see Duke standing still among the milling crowd. Instead, a stall filled with oddments from an interior design shop caught her eye, specifically a roll of gold wallpaper. She picked it up, feeling a flicker of warmth through her body. Her eyes drank the gold as she stroked the raised scrolls.

'You can have that for five dollars,' the girl said.

That evening Ula painted the outline of Mary onto the wallpaper. Night after night, once the baby was settled and Mike watched television, she retreated to her office to work on her new icon. It was better than working by the railway track. Recklessly she added real gold leaf. It was costly but necessary for the light.

When the icon was finished Ula took it to the tracks, intending to paste it over her first attempt. But she felt sorry for the goldless Mary and left her alone. She smeared the bricks with superglue and smoothed on her poster, turning her back to trains and hoping nobody would notice her. She sprayed clear gloss enamel over the image and waited half an hour and sprayed it again and some time later yet again, giving it as many layers as she could, hoping a hard enamel shell would form. Longevity was her aim.

On the way home there was a storm. Dreading a downpour that would disturb her handiwork, Ula looked up into a sky full of sheet lightning. Thunder drummed through the air and trees and earth. No rain followed. Lightning was inferior to fire and gold, Ula thought. What did that art teacher know? Lightning was icy, soulless, electrical. It lacked the warm yellow ingredient of the sun.

When she got home she sat on the kerb. She couldn't shake the feeling Duke was watching her, smoking, following. She looked up and down her street. She didn't want him creeping up the driveway after she had gone inside and *doing something*. She felt sorry for him, but he wasn't to be trusted.

The Madonna wouldn't last. Someone would spray over it. Knowing this didn't diminish her feeling of satisfaction. She had done what she had set out to do. It was something. On Thursday evening she was sweeping up leaves when Mike came looking for her and said:

'I think I'll go camping with Ross this weekend.'

'Sounds good,' said Ula, picking up arm-loads of dry stuff and dropping it into the wheelbarrow. 'I'll make you some tasty food to take.'

'You always do, Ula.'

Hearing something different in his voice she looked across at him, standing awkwardly close. Above his glasses his brow was ribbed with harried lines, some of which she'd put there. He'd said perhaps the only nice thing that could be said about her right now. Brushing her hands on her shorts she said:

'I know I must be – difficult.'

Ula put her arms around him and felt him slump against her. She stroked his hair.

'You're a good man,' she said, quietly. 'A good father. And – husband.'

After their embrace, Mike straightened. 'Stop all this clearing,' he said. 'I'll do it when we get back.'

On Friday she was astonished to find a picture of her graffiti on the front cover of the *Maroondah Leader*. The headline read '*Mystery of the Ringwood Madonna*'. She glowed with pride. People had noticed. Her graffiti even had a name, like a real piece of art.

She read the article. Some people had said nice things about it. A name caught her eye. The journalist had interviewed the art teacher from the icon course.

'It's a work of some skill,' the art teacher was quoted. 'But people shouldn't be spraying that holy image all over town. Mary is a prototype. Divine. An icon should be properly cared for in a quiet place, not sticking up like a bald gold fist out of the muck. Eventually this graffiti Madonna will be disfigured. And what message does *that* send?'

Actually, Ula was surprised the Madonna had not already been vandalised. She wondered if the taggers and graffitists were so taken with the image – or bemused – that they weren't painting over it.

Her graffiti Mary was – to her – a beautiful lamp in the suburban ugliness. A gift. Subconsciously she'd hoped that by creating Mary she would create beauty inside herself, she could see that now. And she *had* felt warmth when she was painting. Yes. Even joy. Mary's tender eyes looked at her from under veils of madder deep.

In the evening, Tania refused the breast for the first time. Ula watched a movie and drank a mug of sherry. Would Duke know Mike was away? She looked out onto the street, wondering if he was there smoking under the acacia trees, burning matches to his fingertips.

I light fires.
Hail, Mary Theotokos.

The next day Ula woke full of energy, after the best sleep she'd had in months. At Riot Art & Craft in Eastland she purchased two cans of blue spray paint. In the afternoon, she put Tania in a backpack and braved the heat by Mullum Mullum Creek. Ula sat in the shade with her legs in the sun and let Tania crawl among the ants. She gave Tania water from a cup before walking up to Ringwood Station and along the tracks to visit Mary, who was still miraculously untouched. Every day Mary was there was an unexpected thrill for Ula. She wanted to show Tania, but she'd fallen asleep, her head heavy on Ula's shoulder, snoring lightly.

'It's a shame, really,' she said aloud, admiring her own work. The skin was dark and lovely, made of yellow ochre and burnt umber, softly glazed with *terre verte* and highlights hatched lightly here and there. Ultramarine shimmered through the magenta veils. The halo had a hint of vermilion. The unfinished Madonna beside the poster was already fading. Winter rains would wash her away.

Once home, Ula kept checking the street, looking for Duke, smoking and forlorn and unloved. She'd pictured him spying on her so often that she couldn't quite believe he wasn't there. She could sense him. *He hides himself, that little bastard.*

She switched on the bedroom fan and lay in bed, slightly stupid with sherry. She slept deeply, wrapped in a long, uninterrupted dream of Duke setting fire to the paperbark tree outside her window. The fire was beautiful. Its radiance surpassed lightning, even gold.

The moonless air was so dark it felt sticky and tasted of ink. Ula wiped her sweaty palms on her trousers. The Sparkles building loomed near the tracks. The stones ground under her boots. She switched on her headlamp and saw the bricks were the same blue as the spray paint. Good. It was a bit mad, what she was doing – but the art teacher was right: better that she get rid of the image now than have it degraded. She shook the spray can and the moment she pressed the nozzle a voice shot out of the darkness.

'Oi!'

An arm came down heavily, knocking the spray can out of her hand. Ula turned to face her attacker and saw Duke, blinking in the light of her headlamp. He shaded his eyes with his forearm and switched on his Maglite.

'You!' he said in surprise. 'But why?'

Ula didn't know what to say. She was sure the art teacher's words would be meaningless to Duke. He shook his head. When he spoke again, there was real anger in his voice.

'I've been protecting her, you know, I...' he said. He stopped, and drew his lower lip under his teeth.

'I didn't know,' said Ula, awkwardly. 'I thought she might be wrecked and I couldn't bear it – so I came to do it myself. Get rid of it altogether rather than have it disfigured.'

Duke shook his head again and shrugged, as if to say *I just don't get it*. He turned and walked rapidly away. Ula hurried after him and put her hand on his arm. He shook her hand away and she grabbed his arm again.

'Don't,' he said irritably, shrugging her off. He was frowning but she saw a hint of a smile on his lips. He stood still. 'What are you doing?'

'I don't know,' she said, honestly. 'I really don't know but it just feels right.'

Warmly dressed against the cold winds, with Tania toddling beside her in a fur-lined bonnet, Ula purchased tickets at Ringwood Station. A silver train squealed to a halt, noisy and bright. Tania's eyes were huge.

'Yes, darling. That's the train.'

She took Tania into her arms and onto the train, deliberately sitting on the side where she wouldn't have to see the blue curtain behind which Mary once reigned. Tania stood on the seat, plump palms leaving smears on the window. *What's it like for you, having me for a mother?*

The train pulled out and gathered speed and Tania gasped with joy.

'Pitty. Pitty!' she said, pointing out the window.

The sun was shining on a new Ringwood Madonna that completely filled her window. Ula's mouth fell open. The Madonna was bigger than her own had been, painted in broader planes with thick key lines. The colours were in the right places. Red and grey, green and brown, white and black holding the delicate balance between peace and danger, purity and impurity, hope and death. The gold shone. It was bold and simple and eloquent.

Ula gaped, swinging between anger and admiration, until she saw in the bottom right-hand corner, a familiar curling D. She had to smile.

'Yes, Tania. That's Mary,' she whispered, her heart streaming like soft red coral towards her daughter. 'She's for you.'

ACKNOWLEDGEMENTS

Thanks to Martin Hughes and Affirm Press for putting art before commerce and publishing short stories; thanks to Rebecca Starford for precise, ruthless and intuitive editing (I'm sure I could have used one less word there), to Amanda Lohrey and Patrick Holland, and to Dean Gorissen for the cover design.

Special thanks to Ray Swann for pushing me deeper into the story of 'Silver Hands'; to Marguerite Swann, Ruby Williams and Biserka Swann for reading, feedback and child care.

Thanks also to the people who have contributed through warm-hearted support or stimulating conversation (or both) to these pages; Lachie Swann, Fred Swann, Peter Williams, Karen Manton,

Esta Kanellopoulos, Halima Vos, Martin Garrett, Julia Inglis, Tony Esta, Beth Christensen, Victoria Swann, Jean Hare, Penny Horsey, Sue Blaze, the late Barrie Hare, Adrian Anderson, Luke Hunter, Sophie Wise, Ian Hodgeson, Mark Bartolo, Cora Brown, Robert Westcott, Jenny Heslop and Narissa Butler. Also to Sharon Thompson, Kim Billington, Leanne Moraes and Andrew Cramb, for your wisdom at various challenging moments. To Dale, Bek and Lisa at Bekendale's – where notes for many of these stories were written – thanks for great coffee and anecdotes.

Finally, to my own little family: thank you to Amos and Brigita, my daily inspiration, for your love and putting up with a mother sometimes distracted or tired; and to my husband John Hare, whose love and steadfast encouragement makes writing possible.